Our Little Danish Cousin

Luna May Innes

Copyright © 2023 Culturea Editions
Text and cover : © public domain
Edition : Culturea (Hérault, 34)
Contact : infos@culturea.fr
Print in Germany by Books on Demand
Design and layout : Derek Murphy
Layout : Reedsy (https://reedsy.com/)
ISBN : 9791041826070
Légal deposit : July 2023

Our Little Danish Cousin

CHAPTER I

THE DISTINGUISHED VISITOR

"HURTIG! kaere Karen, mit lommetørklæde!"

Fru Oberstinde Ingemann and her little flaxen-haired daughter, Karen, were sitting at their embroidery work in the deep window-seat that made one whole side of the cozy Ingemann living-room overlooking the Botanical Gardens. Between stitches, Karen was watching the rain patter on the little diamond window-panes, now and then pausing to take a quick look at some favorite newly-blossomed flower in the brilliant, long line of window-boxes which bordered the windows "like a long bright ribbon," as Karen said.

The bell rang.

"Hurtig! kaere Karen, mit lommetorklaede!" sounds like something terrible, but Fru Ingemann was only saying in Danish: "Quick, dear Karen, my handkerchief!"

"Thank you, Karen," said the lady, as the fair child replaced the sheer bit of linen in her mother's hand with a pretty courtesy, for Karen was a well-bred little girl.

It was a morning of excitement for Fru Else Ingemann. Two important letters had come to her from over the seas. One had come from Chicago in far-away America, saying that her brother-in-law, the Hon. Oscar Hoffman, was coming once more to pay a visit to dear old Denmark. Mr. Hoffman was an important man in America. He was the president of the "Danish-American National Park" in north Jutland, and it was in his loyal Danish brain that the whole idea of the great Park had originated. It had been his dream to save to the glory of Denmark, for all time to come, a wonderful, wild tract of heather-covered hills where, year by year, thousands of loyal Danish-Americans might meet in the Fatherland, and celebrate America's Independence Day on Danish soil. At last the Park was a reality, and he was coming to make necessary arrangements.

He was bringing his son, Karl, with him, and, while they were to be in Copenhagen, they would spend their time with the Ingemanns. He hoped that the little cousins would become great friends. They would arrive in Copenhagen on Saturday. To-day was Thursday.

The other exciting message came from Fru Ingemann's favorite brother, Hr. Thorvald Svensen. It was postmarked Rome, Italy, and informed her that at last he was coming back to live in his dear old home in Copenhagen, and that he would arrive on that day.

Hr. Svensen had been living in Rome for eight long years, and in those years of persistent, hard work he had finally realized his one great ambition, and become Denmark's greatest sculptor — greatest, at least, since the day of Denmark's beloved Thorvaldsen, whose namesake he was.

To Fru Ingemann there was no more welcome news in all the world. His letter said that he longed to see her and the children once more.

Little Valdemar, who was the sculptor's godson, was wild with joy. "Let me stay home from school to-day, mother!" he implored.

"No, no, Valdemar," firmly answered his mother, as she handed him his school luncheon, a box of delicious smörrebröd. When Valdemar's mother said "No, no," he knew that further protests were useless. So he kissed her and was off, calling back: "Good-bye, mother dear; keep Gudfar Thor until I come home from school, please!"

All that morning Fru Ingemann flew about in happy expectancy, making more cozy the pretty little apartment. Karen could hear her mother, as she worked, singing softly those familiar old lines from Baggesen, the well-known Danish poet:

"Ah, nowhere is the rose so red,

Nowhere so small the thorn,

Nowhere so soft the downy bed

As those where we were born."

Above the patter of the rain came the sound of approaching carriage wheels. Fru Ingemann paused.

"Quick, Karen, — the bell! It may be Uncle Thor!"

And so it proved! All the eight, long, lonesome years since she had last seen this dear brother, years in which she had lost her husband, were quickly forgotten in his great hearty embrace.

"Min kaere Soster!"

"Min kaere Broder!"

Their hearts were so full they could not find words.

Karen, tiptoeing, wanted to fling her tiny arms about her big, yellow-bearded, Viking-like, Uncle Thor's neck, so he lifted the little maid high in his strong arms and kissed her.

"Ah, Karen, min lille skat! How you have grown!" he said affectionately. Soft yellow curls framed her pretty face, and two heavy braids of the same glorious hair hung far down her back. "Why, you were just a little, two-year-old baby when I went away to Rome, and now, I've no doubt, you are dreaming of a boarding-school off in France or Switzerland one of these days!"

But Karen only shook her little blond head and laughed, while Uncle Thor's beauty-loving eye beamed on the dainty little damsel in white embroidered frock, half-hose and slippers, as he settled himself comfortably in the big arm-chair near the great, green-tiled stove, whose top almost touched the living-room ceiling.

"Congratulations, dear brother," said Fru Ingemann. "Why didn't you write us all about the great honor you have brought to the family? I saw in this morning's 'Nationaltidende,' that you have just been appointed Court Painter to His Majesty, the King! It is the greatest honor that can come to a Danish artist. I am so proud of you!"

"It is true," he acknowledged, briefly, "but tell me, sister Else, how are the boys, Aage and Valdemar?"

"Oh, Aage is now a big boy of sixteen, off doing his eight years of compulsory military service in the army. Aage will grow up with astraighter back and a better trained body because of his soldiering days. He will be home for Christmas with us."

"And Valdemar?"

"Valdemar is only thirteen, but he is in his second year at the Metropolitan School, one of the best State Latin Schools in all Denmark. He will be back home at three o'clock. I could hardly get him to consent to go to school at all, this morning, after he was told that his Gudfar Thor was coming."

"And Karen studies with her private tutors, here, at home?"

"Yes, Thorvald, besides learning to be a good little housekeeper, as well. But you must be both hungry and tired. It is nearly twelve o'clock. Come, Karen, help me spread the table with something good for Frokost, for Uncle Thor."

A cloth of snowy damask was quickly spread with various viands and meats; tongue, salad, salmon, anchovies, plates of butter, with trays containing French (white) bread, and other trays full of thin slices of rye bread, which is such a favorite with all Danes. Fru Ingemann then placed a bottle of beer beside Hr. Svensen's plate, and brought in the steaming hot tea, which she herself poured into the delicate cups of that wonderful crystalline ware, the famous Royal Copenhagen porcelain—a set doubly cherished by her as an heirloom in her family for many generations.

Karen, who could herself make delicious tea, loved to gaze at the fascinatingly delicate decoration of the cups, which looked, as she said, "like frost on the window-pane;" but she never was allowed to touch this precious set of old Royal Copenhagen, of which not one piece had yet been broken.

"And smörrebröd, brother?" politely urged Fru Ingemann, for no good Danish housewife would ever think of inviting any one to breakfast without having smörrebröd on the table.

"Thanks, sister Else," replied the hungry artist, who immediately set about thickly spreading butter—famous Danish butter—over a slice of rye bread, as did also Karen and her mother, after which each proceeded to select the particular kind of fish or meat preferred, and, arranging it upon the slice of buttered bread, ate it much as we would a sandwich. Uncle Thor made an especially delicious one for Karen, who had already become a great favorite with him.

Frokost over, Fru Ingemann arose, and, bowing slightly to her brother, said: "Velbekomme!" And Hr. Svensen did the same.

"Tak for Mad, Moder," said Karen courtesying first to her mother and then to her Uncle Thor, and kissing them both — a beautiful old Danish custom.

Uncle Thor was a great lover of flowers. To-day there were beautiful flowers on the table, in the windows, everywhere! In fact, the whole Ingemann apartment seemed overwhelmed with the loveliness of them. Besides the vases, there were little flower-pots galore, all decked in brightly-colored paper, some containing blooming plants, others, little growing trees.

"Ah, Karen, has there been a birthday here?" asked Uncle Thor, in mock surprise. "Run out in the hall and see what came all the way from Naples, Italy, to Frederiksberg-Alle, in Copenhagen, for a good little girl with long pigtails."

Karen came running back with a tiny white kid box in her hand. Opening it, she beheld the most beautiful set imaginable of pale pinkcorals. She just couldn't wait to put the necklace on before hugging her dear old Uncle Thor, who himself had to fasten the pretty chain around her slender little neck for her.

"Yes, Uncle Thor, we had a splendid time, and mother gave us chocolate, tea and cakes, and this is what all the boys and girls at my party yesterday sang:

"'London Bridge is broken down,

Gold is won and bright renown,

Shields resounding, war-horns sounding,

Hild is shouting in the din,

Arrows singing,

Mailcoats ringing,

Odin makes our Olaf win.'"

Karen had hardly finished singing her song describing the days of old, when there had been a mighty encounter on London Bridge between the Danes and King Olaf the Saint, ending in the burning of the bridge, when there came a sudden great clatter and uproar on the stairs, with the loud barking of a dog, and the sound of a boy's heavy boots, and Valdemar burst into the room.

"Oh, my dear, dear Gudfar Thor!" he exclaimed, throwing his arms tight round his uncle's neck.

"Why, Valdemar, you are the very image of your father!" exclaimed Hr. Svensen. "Don't you think so, sister Else?" he questioned, as he gazed admiringly at the sturdy, big frame, rumpled flaxen hair, and the merry twinkle in the honest blue Danish eyes of his godson.

"Oh, yes, Thorvald, Valdemar certainly is the image of his father. The King thinks so, too," agreed Fru Ingemann.

"King Frederik? Why, how is that, sister? Has the king never forgotten Valdemar?" questioned Hr. Svensen in surprise.

"Oh, Thorvald, you know the King's wonderful memory. It never fails him. And you must remember the great friendship that always existed between my dear husband and King Frederik, from the days when, as boys together, they went through the Military College; and later both were recruits in the same regiment, and had to do sentry duty, turn about, outside his grandfather's palace. Only the other day, Valdemar came bounding into the house, overjoyed, to tell me that he had just passed their Majesties, King Frederik and Queen Lowisa, out walking on the Langelinie,entirely unattended, and that, when he doffed his cap to the King, his Majesty immediately returned his salute, with a friendly smile!"

"But, sister Else, how do you know that King Frederik thinks Valdemar the image of his father? I don't understand," persisted Hr. Svensen, perplexed.

"We know!" Fru Ingemann spoke softly as she.

"Valdemar was only a little child when his father died," she continued. "His father had always taught Valdemar to love the King, and he does so with all his boyish little heart. An accident, a broken arm, soon afterwards put the child in the Queen Lowisa Children's Hospital, where, as you know, King Frederik makes a monthly visit to cheer the little sufferers. The King loves children. They say that not one little baby-face ever escapes him, and that he even notes each child's improvement from time to time.

"Valdemar, in his little cot near the door, heard the nurses saying: 'The King comes to-day!'

"His little mind was all expectation. Finally, the King arrived. Valdemar was the first little patient to see him enter, silk hat in his hand as usual. Sick as he was, the boy drew himself quickly from out of the covers, stood up in the middle of his bed, and saluted his King with a low bow, so low that his forehead almost touched his pillow. The King paused in surprise at Valdemar's cot and spoke:

"'My child, why do you do that? Why do you salute me?'

"'Because I like you! You are the King!'

"They say that the King looked into the child's face a moment, drew his hand to his eyes, lost in thought, then, turning quickly to Prince Christian, who accompanied him, exclaimed with a smile:

"'Du ligner din Fader! Oh, vilde jeg onske at din Fader levede! Gid Legligheden maa komme til at hjälpe denne opvagte Dreng, for min käre gamle Ven Ingemann's Skyld!'

"Then, placing his hand on the child's golden locks, he spoke tenderly: 'Yes, little Valdemar Ingemann, I am the King. Alwaysremember that your father and I were great friends,' and he passed on.

"Valdemar has never forgotten that moment. He never will. You and the King are the two great heroes of the world in his eyes."

"Where is he now? Come, Valdemar! Tell me all about what you like most to read," called Uncle Thor.

"Oh, Uncle Thor, I love to read in the old Sagas and Chronicles all about the mighty sea-fights of the Vikings, and about the glorious battles of the Valdemars, in the books that Aage left me. They make me want to be a soldier. Then I love to read everything about Linnæus, who loved the trees and the flowers and the whole outdoors just as I do. But, best of all, I'd rather become a famous sculptor like my Godfather Thor! I'd like that better than anything else in all the world! See, Uncle Thor, I've modelled some little things already. Here is one,—my Great Dane, Frederik,—and here is a stork, and here is a little Viking ship. They're not very good, but—"

"Oh, min lille Billedhugger!" interrupted Hr. Svensen, with feeling, as he took the little toy animals from Valdemar to examine them. "This is not half bad work. But what have you done them in, my boy?"

"In pie-paste!" laughed his mother. "I have to hide the pie-paste when I'm baking, to keep Valdemar from slipping it off to use for modelling!"

"Valdemar, you shall have some modelling clay. Thorvaldsen once made the Lion of Lucerne in butter. I must tell you that story some day," said Hr. Svensen, as he patted his little nephew's head affectionately.

There was a sharp ring at the bell.

Karen flew to the door, then back to her mother, excitedly exclaiming: "A box and a letter for you, mother!"

Fru Ingemann tore the note open and read: "Will be expelled if it occurs again!" The words swam before her eyes.

"Oh, Valdemar, my son, come explain all this to me at once! It is from your Latin teacher. Surely there is some mistake. It is not like my boy!"

Meantime Karen had opened the box, and displayed a most laughable clay caricature of Valdemar's Latin teacher, with the word "TEACHER" scratched underneath in large letters. She burst out giggling. Even Uncle Thor's look of mock horror soon gave way before the cleverly done effigy, and he laughed. He had been a boy once himself, and it was funny.

"Well, that's exactly the way teacher looks!" vehemently protested Valdemar in self-justification. "Indeed he does. Ask Hendrik or any of the boys. None of us like him one bit, and at recess to-day Hendrik drew chalk cartoons of teacher all over the blackboard, and said: 'Oh, Valdemar, you'd never dare do it in clay!'

"'Yes, I would dare do it in clay!' I answered him, and then, mother, — I did it. But I didn't mean Hr. Professor Christiansen to see it. I'm glad school's over for all summer on Friday!"

Even Valdemar's mother had to laugh, as Uncle Thor took the offending statuette in his hand to give it a closer examination, for it was as irresistibly funny as it was clever.

"Brilliant, Valdemar!" he exclaimed. "Your work has merit. Work hard enough, my boy, and you may become a great artist, some day. You have the talent. Come over to my studio to-morrow morning. I'll help you a little with your modelling, and then, after luncheon with me, I will take you through the Thorvaldsen Museum. Would you like that? And, by the way, I think there is something nice for you in my trunk. Now I am due at the Royal Palace. I must go and pay my respects to the King. He will be expecting me."

"Oh, Uncle Thor, I'll be there!" called out Valdemar. "Good-bye, Uncle Thor, good-bye!"

CHAPTER II

COPENHAGEN

SUMMER bursts suddenly in Copenhagen. First, winter, with its deep snows, its fogs and frosts and thaws; then a few days of showers and a few of sunshine, Blinkeveir the Danes call this showery weather; and then, all at once, the bare trees throw out their tender green foliage and the spring flowers burst into life! The long cold winter is over. Even then, there sometimes come dense sea-mists which envelop Denmark's capital, and only vanish with the sun's warm rays. So Copenhageners have a popular weather saying:

"'Monday's weather till mid-day is the week's weather till Friday,

Friday's weather is Sunday's weather,

Saturday has its own weather."

Saturday's weather fortunately proved ideal, a rare June day. Copenhagen's beautiful Public Gardens and Parks were all aglow with fragrant, blossoming spring flowers. Valdemar's school was at last over.

"Now to the woods!" he cried in joy. "And, mother dear, can't we keep Cousin Karl all summer with us up at our country place on theStrandvej, while Uncle Oscar has to be away in Jutland attending to that Park of his? But I should like to be there with him when they have their big American Fourth of July celebration, and see them raise their great Star Spangled Banner over our beloved flag! Wouldn't you, Karl? I've heard about the American 'Fourth,' with the Stars and Stripes waving everywhere, and of the army manœuvres and big times they have over there in the States on that historic day! But Denmark's never had anything like it before, has she, Uncle Thor?"

They were in Fru Ingemann's pretty dining-room having their twelve o'clock little frokost of tea and smörrebröd, this happy little party of six, for the American relatives had arrived.

Early that morning, Valdemar and his Uncle Thor had hurried to the dock to meet the steamer, "and, but for Uncle Oscar's waving handkerchief, and his good memory for faces, we might have missed them entirely," explained Valdemar, who was delighted with this first acquaintance with his new American cousin.

With the first warm spring day, half of Copenhagen whitewashes her town house windows against the sun's hot rays, and prepares to migrate farther north, to the famous Strandvej, where soft breezes from the blue Sound play all day over the broad sandy beach, and rustle through the leaves of the beech-trees in the Deer Park near by. Rich and poor alike own their own villas, country houses or little cottages, as the case may be, and these thickly dot the beautiful east Sound Shore all the way from Copenhagen to Elsinore, for great is the Dane's love of at ligger på Landet.

Like all the rest, through wise and careful planning, Fru Ingemann had her little country place on the beautiful east Shore, where each summer Karen and Valdemar took long walks through the glorious beech-woods, went swimming, boating and bathing, made their own flower-gardens and dug in the ground to their hearts' content. By the end of each short, happy summer, they were both as tanned and brown as the baskets of beech-nuts they gathered and brought back with them for the winter.

"We will have great times, if only Cousin Karl can come up for the summer with us!" begged little Karen.

"I'll think about it," was the only promise they could get out of Uncle Oscar for the moment. "I'm sure Karl would like it, but I'm not ready to decide anything just now."

"If I'm not mistaken, the first thing Karl wants is to see some of the sights of Copenhagen," said Hr. Svensen, as they were leaving the breakfast table. "Suppose we all go together and give him a bird's-eye view of Copenhagen and the Harbor from the top of the Round Tower! How's that, Karl?"

"Great! Can't we start right away?" said the little American, for Karl was a typical little Chicago boy, eager-minded and anxious to take in everything at once.

"And the Thorvaldsen Museum, Uncle Thor? Can't we go back there again to-day?" urged Valdemar, for the wondrous beauty of Thorvaldsen's masterpieces still filled all his thoughts. On the way home from the Museum, the previous day, he had listened to fascinating stories told him by his godfather, stories about the "Lion of Lucerne," and about the little peasant boy who loved art, and worked hard, and finally became one of the world's greatest sculptors. Valdemar couldn't forget Thorvaldsen's lovely "Guardian Angel," or his wonderful figure of "Christ," with its bowed head and arms outstretched in benediction, or the heavenly beauty of his "Angel of the Baptism kneeling at Christ's feet." Never, thought Valdemar, had he seen anything half so beautiful in all his life! Then, there were mighty gods and heroes, and graceful nymphs. "And only think," continued Valdemar, "when Thorvaldsen was just a little boy eleven years old,—three years less than I am—he so loved his drawing and modelling that his father, who was a poor Icelandic ship-builder and carver of figureheads, placed him in school at the Academy of Arts, where he won prize after prize, not stopping until he had gained even the great gold medal, together with the travelling scholarship which took him to Italy to study. There he worked hard day by day, from early dawn till dark without stopping. No wonder the great Museum is completely filled with masterpieces from his hand!"

"Valdemar, my boy, you, too, shall enter as a student at the Academy next fall, if your work during the summer continues to show the talent and improvement that will justify my sending you. But that means you must work hard. I leave next week for my summer studio up at Skagen, but, until I go, you shall have a lesson each day, if you like, and more lessons up there all summer long, if you will come, for there is no little boy in all the world I would rather help than you, my Valdemar."

"Oh, Uncle Thor!" cried Valdemar, throwing his arms around his godfather's neck, wild with joy. "I will begin to-morrow. And do you really mean that I am to study at the Academy?"

"Yes, my little artist," answered Hr. Svensen. "And now let us start at once and see some of Copenhagen's sights."

"And will Fru Oberstinde not accompany us?" politely inquired Mr. Hoffman, of his sister-in-law.

Danish wives and widows are given the same titles their husbands bear, so that Fru Ingemann, who was the widow of a Colonel, or "Oberst," in the King's army, was often addressed as "Oberstinde," or "Coloneless."

"Not to-day, thank you. Karen and I will wait for you at home," said Fru Ingemann, smiling as she observed the big book in her child's hands. "You see what Karen is reading, Hans Christian Andersen's fascinating 'Billedbog unden Billeder.' Be sure to be back in time for dinner," she called as the party set off.

"God Dag," said the tram conductor politely as they entered. Karl smiled. Then he began to ask questions, for he had never crossed the ocean before, and never before had he seen any city like Copenhagen. Chicago certainly had its broad avenues, parks and boulevards, great skyscrapers and fine buildings; but Chicago had never dreamed of permitting its one great canal to run right up through the city streets, among the office buildings and houses, with all its shipping, launches and water-craft, as the Copenhagen canals all seemed to do in the friendliest possible fashion.

"Copenhagen must look much more like Amsterdam than like Athens, father. I can't see why it is called the 'Athens of the North.' I don't see any Greek-looking buildings here," protested Karl.

"Yes," agreed Karl's father, who had once lived in Denmark long years ago. "Copenhagen may look much more like Amsterdam, Karl; but, while you will not see Greek buildings here, nevertheless the title of 'Athens' comes justly, not only because of Copenhagen's charming position on the borders of the Sound at the entrance to the Baltic, giving the city a great advantage commercially, and because of its beautifully wooded environs, but particularly on account of its splendid libraries, art galleries, museums and great university and schools, which rank among the best to be found anywhere in Europe. Before we reach the Round Tower we will doubtless get a view of some of these."

"Fa' vel," said the tram conductor, bowing pleasantly to them as they got off at their destination.

Karl laughed outright. "Dear me! In Chicago car conductors are given prizes for politeness, but I must say, none of them have ever yet reached the point of saying 'farewell' to you as you leave. I'm glad they don't. Gee! We'd never get anywhere in Chicago if we stopped for all that."

"Half of Copenhagen seems to be out on the streets to-day," remarked Mr. Hoffman, who had not been back to Denmark's beautiful capital for so long that he had forgotten what a large city it was. "Look, I believe that must be the New Picture Gallery, isn't it?"

"You are right," replied Hr. Svensen. "Half the charm of Copenhagen must be traced to her museums and rich art treasures. Shall we give the boys a peep inside?"

"Oh, yes!" exclaimed both boys at once, for Karl had pleasant memories of Saturday afternoons he had spent studying all the fine exhibits in the Museum of the Art Institute of Chicago. They had soon climbed the broad granite steps, and were walking through the long corridors and halls filled with great paintings, each bearing the artist's name on the frame.

"The New Picture Gallery affords a good opportunity for studying Danish pictorial art, just as the New Glyptothek does for studying Danish sculpture," said Hr. Svensen, as they were leaving.

"What canal is that?" asked Karl. "It certainly is a pretty one, with that beautiful promenade and park along one side."

"Yes, that is Holmen's Canal, one of the finest in Copenhagen," answered Hr. Svensen. It was full of ships and other water-craft. "And that marble building which looks like an Etruscan tomb is the Thorvaldsen Museum, one of the principal attractions of Copenhagen. We shall have to take another day for that. But, just to please Valdemar, we will spend a moment inside the church where Thorvaldsen's 'Christ,' the 'Angel of the Baptism' and 'The Twelve Apostles' are all standing in the places for which they were designed."

"The Danes have accomplished much more in sculpture than in painting, haven't they, Uncle Thor?" Valdemar asked.

"Yes, you are quite right, Valdemar. Denmark, as yet, has produced no painter to compare with Thorvaldsen."

They paused a moment at the New Raadhus-plads, with its castellated roof, and paved semicircle in front, and again, near by, at the New City Hall.

"What an attractive part of Copenhagen this is," remarked Karl, as he observed the many broad, fine, well-kept Pladser, with their electric cars gliding noiselessly back and forth with American celerity. "Copenhagen seems to me a much cleaner, prettier city than Chicago, father. Don't you think so? But where are its beggars? We've not yet seen one."

Hr. Svensen was quick to answer that they were not likely to see one. That Copenhagen, with a population of nearly five hundred thousand, has a pauper element of less than three per cent. "For the Danes are naturally a thrifty, industrious people, more than half of whom are farmers, and many also go to sea in ships," explained Hr. Svensen.

They took a tram down Stormgade over a bridge to the island of Slotsholmen, with its famous Fruit and Flower Market, where jolly-looking women with quaint headdresses were selling their wares; then over another bridge intoKongens Nytorv, the King's New Market.

"Here we are in a different world from that which we just left," said Hr. Svensen. They had reached a large Square, a great centre of life and bustle, from which thirteen busy streets radiated. Through the trees in the centre of this great open space the statue of a king was seen, and red omnibuses crept slowly along on each side of the tram line. Here they saw the Royal Theatre, the famous Tivoli Gardens, and the beautiful old Palace of Charlottenburg, close to an inlet of the sea, which reached right into the Square with all its shipping, so that masts and sails and shops and buildings took on the same friendly aspect that they have in Holland.

"But I don't see any 'skyscrapers,' Uncle Thor, like we have in Chicago, sometimes twenty stories high! Where are they?" inquired the little American.

"In a moment or so, Karl, I will show you two 'skyscrapers' that will amuse you!" said Hr. Svensen. "But, look! here is a lively scene for us first."

They were passing the Copenhagen fish-market, or Gammelstrand, as it is called, where the fish are sold alive, after having been kept in large perforated boxes in the canal.

"Now look, Karl! how's that for a skyscraper?"

They were looking at the tall tower of the Bors, or Exchange, one hundred and fifty feet high, with its upper part formed by four great dragons whose tails were so intertwined and twisted together, high up in the air, that they gradually tapered to a point, like a spire against the sky.

Then there was another tower which interested Karl. It was on the Church of Our Redeemer. Circled by a long spiral stairway of three hundred and ninety-seven steps of gleaming brass, which wound round and round and up and up to the very top of the sharp cone, this tower gave the persevering climber a good panoramic view over Copenhagen.

"But not so good a view as we can get from the top of the Round Tower," said Hr. Svensen. "Here we are now."

They were glad to quit the jostling crowds on the streets,—throngs of busy shoppers, students in cap and gown, sightseers, and, to-day, bright-coated soldiers at every turn. The soldiers were arriving in Copenhagen by hundreds every day now, they were told, in order to be ready, Monday morning, to welcome King Haakon of Norway, who was expected to arrive by ship.

"Oh, Uncle Thor, will you or Uncle Oscar not bring us down to the city, Monday, and let us see King Haakon drive past?" cried out both boys at once.

"Yes, boys," said Mr. Hoffman, "I will be glad to bring you. I leave for Jutland in the afternoon, Monday, and that will give me my last chance to see a little more of Copenhagen."

At last they were in the Round Tower, and felt themselves slowly ascending. Up and up, and round and round and round on an inclined plane, they went—past curious niches in the wall, containing ancient monuments covered with Runic inscriptions; past a door leading to the university library, with its valuable collection of rare Icelandic manuscripts; slowly, on and on, until finally they reached the very top with its observatory, once the home of the great astronomer, Tycho Brahe.

"Peter the Great once drove a coach and four to the top of this very same tower," volunteered Karl. "I've read all about that at school in Chicago. What a splendid view of the city we are having. It is all spires, and red roofs and gables built stairway fashion, isn't it?"

"And how beautiful and sparkling the waters of the harbor look, all alive with ships, great and small," said Valdemar. "It certainly is a splendid seaport!"

Far away, the Baltic, blue as the Bay of Naples, shimmered in the bright sunlight; and close at hand, at the various wharves, merchantmen, with valuable cargoes from far countries, were loading and unloading. It was a scene of busy life. The boys counted the flags of many different nations. No wonder the city had been named Merchant's Haven, or Kjöbenhavn.

"What a good view of the coast of Sweden we get up here," said Valdemar. "And north of us lies Elsinore, the scene of Hamlet's tragedy. And, Karl, I'm sure that, on a clearer day, we could see Rugen, the German island, where, one day long ago, the Kaiser sat on the top of the cliff four hundred feet high, and watched the famous sea-fight between the Swedes and the Danes. But I don't like to talk about Germany. I'm glad that Aage is a soldier. Some day he will help us get Schleswig back again!" said patriotic little Valdemar. "And, only think, some of the geography books have even dared to call the North Sea the German Ocean! Kiel Harbor, now bristling with German war-ships, once belonged to Denmark, and so did the whole Baltic!"

"Yes, and once the Danes were ruling half of England, Ireland, and Scotland, and they even gained a foothold in Normandy," said little Cousin Karl by way of consolation.

"And the Germans once stood in terror of our great Vikings, who lorded it over the seas in every direction!" added Valdemar, with growing enthusiasm. "Their graves may be seen on both sides of the North Sea today. And wasn't it here, Uncle Thor, when an unusually severe winter had bridged the Baltic, that the Swedish king, Karl Gustav, led his army, horse, foot and guns, over the frozen seas where no one had dared to cross before, and finally took Copenhagen? But Denmark and Sweden are at peace now."

"I'm glad that they are," replied Karl, "and that Norway and Denmark are, too, or we might not see King Haakon next Monday!"

"Come!" said Uncle Thor. "Let us hurry home now, before we are late to dinner. It is a wonderful old tower, having survived both fires and bombardments. Once Copenhagen was fortified with a wall and a moat, for Denmark's capital has passed through many vicissitudes, but in these peaceful days they both have been turned into parks for the people."

Dinner had been awaiting the hungry sightseers for some time when they reached home.

When they had all gathered about the dinner table, it was plain that there was some great secret in the air. Fru Ingemann's face wore a bright smile, in spite of the late dinner, and little Karen held herself with an air of supreme importance, her cheeks bright, and her blue eyes dancing with suppressed excitement.

"Great news, Brother Thorvald!" began Fru Ingemann, handing him a great white envelope bearing the arms of His Majesty, King Frederik. "When Karen and I were quietly studying the recipe book, and thinking of the dinner far more than of kings, the bell rang sharply, and, lo and behold! there stood the King's royal Jaeger—in green uniform, three-cornered hat and all—inquiring for you, brother!

"'His Majesty, the King, sends this message to Hr. Professor Svensen,' he said with a gracious bow, and, again bowing low, departed. Karen and I, as you can well imagine, have been guessing everything possible and impossible ever since, and given up in despair, waiting for you to explain it all to us yourself, Thorvald."

By this time, Valdemar's and Karen's eyes were bulging wild with curiosity, and even Mr. Hoffman's face showed extreme interest. What could it be?

"I am summoned to the Royal Palace Tuesday at eleven o'clock," explained Hr. Svensen, "to begin immediate work upon a statue of His Royal Highness, the Crown Prince Olaf of Norway, who has graciously consented to give me a few sittings during his short visit in Denmark."

When Uncle Thor had finished reading, he passed the great white envelope, headed "Royal Palace," with its interesting contents, over to his sister and the children. Never before had the King's Jaeger come to Fru Ingemann's little apartment out on Frederiksberg-Alle!

Valdemar was the first to speak.

"Oh, Uncle Thor! I wonder if dear little Prince Olaf will pose with his beautiful big dog! He is never without him, you know. And oh,dear! Uncle Thor, can't you take me along with you to mix your clay — keep it damp for you, and just do lots of things you'd like done? I want to go with you so much, Uncle Thor, to watch you work! I know I could help you ever so much, if only you would just take me!" urged the little embryo sculptor of the now great one.

"My dear little Valdemar," said Uncle Thor with much tenderness in his voice, "you are very welcome to go with me to the RoyalPalace 'to watch me work.' But, first, I want to watch you work. Watching me will not do you much good, my little artist, until you have done more work, yourself! This summons may delay my leaving for my summer studio, up at Skagen, until the end of the week, and I am willing to give half of every day, until I go, to teaching you. Now try to have some work ready to show me by to-morrow. I will bring you more modelling clay when you have used up what you have here. In fact, I will bring you some of my own tools, and some casts for you to use as studies. Perhaps I can fit up a real little studio right here in your own home for you. I want to see what talent you have, Valdemar."

"Oh, brother, how very good of you!" exclaimed Fru Ingemann. "Valdemar must work very hard. He has talent, I feel sure."

They had all finished their soup, a kind of very sweet gruel with vegetables, and a dish of ham was then placed before Fru Ingemann, who carved it, and passed around the slices, beginning with her nearest guest. Fish, preserves, and stewed fruits were served with it. Then followed Rodgrod, a kind of jelly to which the juice of different fruits had been added, tea and coffee, and the little dinner ended with the same ceremony as breakfast. Karl tried to suppress a smile as Valdemar and little Karen courtesied to their mother and uncles, as they said politely: "Thank you for the food," and went around and kissed them.

"My son," said Karl's father, reprovingly, "I like these beautiful old Danish customs. I only wish you and all our little American boys and girls had more of this feeling of gratitude."

"Come, Karl," called Valdemar, "and see my beautiful Della Robbia 'Singing Boys,' that Uncle Thor brought to me all the way from Italy!"

As the boys disappeared, the two men withdrew to the smoking-room for a chat over their cigars, while Fru Ingemann busied herself assembling all the "birthday flowers" into the front window overlooking the avenue, according to an old-time custom in Copenhagen. Then she tucked little Karen snugly in bed with a great pillow propped up against her feet to keep the drafts off, for the early June day had grown suddenly cooler towards night.

CHAPTER III

"HURRAH FOR KING FREDERIK!"

"VALDEMAR, tell me! What is a real king like?" exclaimed Karl, as both boys sprang quickly out of bed bright and early Monday morning. "Is a real king something like a President, only he's all gorgeous with flashing decorations, and a sword and helmet, — like the pictures of Napoleon and the German Emperor?"

"Karl, you must have been dreaming about kings! I can't tell you whether a king is like a President or not, for I've never seen a President," said Valdemar. "But I am sure of one thing, and that is that our King isn't one bit like the German Emperor! King Frederik just looks like the very best king Denmark ever had, and that is what he really is!"

"Oh, excuse me, Valdemar. I forgot that you don't love the Germans. But does King Frederik come riding a great prancing charger with an arched neck and — "

"You'll soon enough see for yourself how the King looks, Karl. Oh, there's Uncle Thor! Uncle Thor, how long before we can start?" cried Valdemar, who was himself almost as excited over the prospect of seeing two great kings at once, as was Karl. Valdemar had never seen King Haakon of Norway, son of his own dear King, and, although Karl, who was nearly twelve years old, had seen two Presidents, and gone once with his father to the White House in Washington, he had never seen a real live king in all his short life.

"Oh, father dear!" he cried, "when can we start? There! I think I heard a bugle! Oh, do let's go!"

"We will start before very long, Karl, but not until you boys have had your tea and bread. And, if I'm not mistaken, I heard Valdemar's uncle say that he was to have a good lesson in drawing this morning. King Haakon's ship does not arrive in Copenhagen harbor before almost noon, so there will be plenty of time."

"Yes, I do want my lesson!" said Valdemar, as they finished their cups of hot tea. "I'm ready, Uncle Thor," he called out, as he saw his uncle passing.

Valdemar was in a very happy frame of mind this fine June morning, for his uncle had praised his work of the day before. Valdemar had modelled a half life-sized figure of his Great Dane, Frederik, and, to his great surprise, Uncle Thor had not only said that it was good, but had told his mother that it undeniably showed evidence of real talent. Nothing could please Valdemar more.

Saturday's sightseeing had given them all a taste for more. Fortunately, Karl had brought his bicycle with him from Chicago, and so the two boys followed on their wheels, while Fru Ingemann took her brother, Mr. Hoffman, and little Karen all in a carriage, and drove the length of the beautiful Shore Road, called the Langelinie, or Long Line,—Copenhagen's fashionable drive, that stretches for miles along the sea. The place was gay with Sunday crowds,—walking, riding, wheeling, driving,—all out enjoying the warm June sunshine, as well as the bracing sea-breeze.

When they reached the quaint old Citadel, they left the carriage and strolled about the earthworks, viewing the monument made from the guns of the wrecked Dannebrog, a ship fitly named after the Danish flag. Promenaders thronged the Shore Road at this point, gazing at the shipping of all nations which here covered the Sound, and off into the dim distance, at the shores of Sweden.

Karl thought that his Aunt Else must have hosts of little friends, for all the small boys bowed, and the little girls courtesied so prettily, as she passed. But Fru Ingemann explained to him that it was only a custom of all well-bred Danish children to bow and courtesy to their elders, and then she told him how, every spring at Paaske, or Easter, as we call it, this beautiful Shore Road is thronged all day long with gay crowds all decked out in their Paaske finery, as it is again later at Store Bededag, or Great Praying Day, on the fourth Friday after Easter.

From here they drove out to the old Castle of Rosenborg, with its fine garden where little children were playing about the statued-form of their beloved story-teller, Hans Christian Andersen; and then straight home again, passing, on their way, the royal residential quarter, Amalienborg, which forms a great open Square, adorned with the beautiful Marble Church, and, in the centre of the Square, with a statue of King Frederik V.

"Now we're off!" said Uncle Thor, as Valdemar finished a very good drawing lesson, for Karl and his father, and Karen and her mother were already waiting.

At first the electric tram simply flew. But, as they approached the down-town section of the city, its way was often blocked by the dense crowds, who, like themselves, were coming to witness the arrival of Copenhagen's honored royal guest, His Majesty, King Haakon of Norway.

"Norroway-over-the-Foam, as it was once called," laughed Fru Ingemann, "is a land of beauty which we must all visit some day. It is so many, many times the size of our little Denmark that it makes us feel, by comparison at least, a very small country indeed."

"But Denmark occupies more space on the map than either Belgium or Holland," said Valdemar.

"And Denmark is nearly twice the size of Massachusetts," added Karl. "But, oh! Just do look at the terrible crowds!—and right here is where we get off! Father says 'Come!'"

All at once they were thrust into the vast crowd. All Copenhagen seemed suddenly to have poured by thousands forth into the streets, and the flags of Norway and Denmark floated everywhere side by side.

"If only we can make the opposite side of the street!" said Uncle Thor, nervously looking about him in every direction, "we shall be safe, for right up there, on the second floor of that building, is my friend's office, from the window of which we are to view the royal procession. Ah! we're safe now!"

No sooner had they taken their positions in the large open window, than they heard, in the distance, a cannon's loud report. It was followed by a salute of guns and loud cheering.

"There!" said both boys at once. "That means that King Haakon has landed, and is now on his way here!"

The cheering sounded nearer and nearer, and the cannon continued to boom.

"Forty guns!" said Valdemar, who had been counting. "Forty guns is Denmark's royal salute. Karen dear, can you see?"

"Yes, thank you, brother," said the child, whose feet were fairly dancing with so much excitement. "But look! They are clearing the street! The people are being made to keep back on the sidewalks. Listen! That is our glorious old National Hymn that the splendid Royal Guards are now playing. The King must be near! Listen, Karl! Oh, isn't it all thrilling!"

Nearer and nearer sounded the familiar strains.

"It is splendid, Karen," conceded Karl, "but I'd like the Star Spangled Banner just as well, and, besides, I guess a king's no bigger'n a President! Oh, look!" But it was only an advance guard of mounted police.

"I'm glad, mother, that our window has the largest flag in town flying from it," said Valdemar. "I just do hope the King will look up here and see it! Listen! Now the people are beginning to cheer right down here under our very window! And the men are doffing their hats!"

"Hurrah! Hurrah! Hurrah!" cheered the loyal thousands, as the scarlet-coated King's Guard came in view.

"Oh!" gasped Karen, with a long-drawn breath of delight. "Oh! isn't it glorious! Hear the bugle! And here come the mounted Hussars with their little red capes fastened on one shoulder, and swords flashing! How splendidly they ride!"

"Mother, I'm going to wave my own flag when the King's carriage passes!" cried patriotic little Valdemar. "If King Frederik will only look up! Don't you hope he will, Karl? Oh! there's his carriage now! Yes, he sees my flag waving! He's looking! I'm going to cheer! Hurrah for King Frederik!"

The King heard and raised his head. His eyes fell directly upon Valdemar's bright face, as had been the case that long ago day, in the Children's Hospital. King Frederik smiled, bowed, and gave the lad a military salute of recognition. King Haakon was seated beside King Frederik, but

Valdemar did not see him. In the following carriage were the two queens, Queen Maud of Norway, and their own beloved Danish Queen Lowisa, with little Crown Prince Olaf, of Norway, seated between them; but Valdemar saw only King Frederik.

"Mother! He knew me!" cried Valdemar, as the brilliant procession passed slowly out of sight, and the music, whose strains came faintly back to them, had changed from Denmark's "Kong Christian" to the Norwegian National Hymn in honor of King Haakon.

CHAPTER IV

UP THE SOUND TO HAMLET'S CASTLE

"MOTHER dear, how fine and cool the sea-breeze feels!" exclaimed Valdemar, as the little Sound steamer puffed along over the bright Baltic waves, past the big merchant-ships on the blue Sound, making many stops on its way up towards historic old Elsinore, the spot made famous by Shakespeare.

Uncle Oscar had departed three days before, going directly to the Jutland Park, to begin preparations for the entertaining of the thousands of loyal Danish-American visitors, expected to arrive in time for the Fourth celebration, and Fru Ingemann had given him her promise to meet him there, with the three children, for that great event.

For it had not taken Fru Ingemann long to decide that Uncle Oscar's plan for the summer was best. Summer days are long, but few, in Denmark,—the winters cold and stormy,—and Karen and Valdemar needed the trip as much as did Karl, she told herself. So the little party of four were already on their way north, to see for themselves all the wonders and beauties of Jutland, of which Karl's father had been telling them.

Once Fru Ingemann had decided, the days fairly flew. Valdemar wanted to start at once. But there was all the packing to be done—of things to be left, and things to be taken—and the flat to be closed for at least several months.

Karen, who had never before been farther from home than their own little villa up on the Strandvej, was overjoyed and danced busily about, saving her mother steps in a thousand different ways; while Valdemar and Karl surprised Fru Ingemann by getting out ladders, buckets and brushes, and nicely whitewashing all the flat windows, which was really being very useful indeed.

"Aunt Else, why is our steamer so awfully crowded with people? Are the Sound boats always like this?" asked Karl, who could hardly turn his chair around without knocking into some one.

"Yes, Karl, it's like this every year at 'Deer-Park-time.' The huge crowds are as eager as ourselves to leave Copenhagen with the first warm day and flee to Skoven, for we Danes love our beautiful woods. With the first bursting of the beech-buds, everybody asks everybody else: 'Have you been in the woods yet?' And then by thousands—young and old—they flock to our beloved beech-woods. Those who cannot find room on the boats take the first train, or carriage, or cycle, or car, or even foot it—any way at all in order to reach the Deer Park, for that is where most of them go. After we make a stop there, we shall have plenty of room on our boat, Karl. Look! We are passing Charlottenlund, the Crown Prince's palace. You can see it up among those fine old trees."

"Then, Aunt Else," asked Karl, "isn't 'Deer-Park-time' something like our American 'Indian Summer,' only that it comes in the spring? It's your finest part of spring, and our best part of fall, when every one wants to live out of doors. Isn't that it?"

"That's just right, Karl," laughed Fru Ingemann. "And a little Danish boy would feel almost as badly not to be taken to the beech-woods when 'Deer-Park-time' comes, as would a little English boy if he got no plum pudding on Christmas day, or a little Scotch boy without his currant bun on New Year's Day, or a nice little American boy like you, Karl, if he couldn't have any firecrackers for his Fourth of July celebration. But here we are stopping at the Deer Park now. Half the people are getting off."

Valdemar's eyes looked far beyond the disembarking crowds landing at the pier. He saw only the dark pine trees in the distance, straight and tall, suggesting to his imaginative mind giant masts for Viking ships. Many a fine day had he spent tramping through those tree-shaded walks with his mother, while she told him wonderful stories about Denmark's great heroes of old.

"In America, we like to go to the woods, too," said Karl; "but not just to walk and walk all day. We like to play ball, or climb the trees for nuts, or keep doing something all the time. Do you ever do anything but just walk, in your woods?"

"Sometimes, on a warm summer's evening in the woods, we sing some beautiful old hymn, like Grundtwig's:

"'For Danes have their home where the fair beeches grow,

By shores where forget-me-nots cluster,

And fairest to us, by cradle and grave,

The blossoming field by the swift-flowing wave.'

There are no people in all the world, Karl, who have the same simple love for their trees, as do the Danes," explained his Aunt Else.

"There, Karl, we are starting again," said Valdemar.

The beautiful Deer Park, with its masses and pyramids of green foliage, followed the Sound-Shore for five miles before the steamer had left it behind. The boat kept close to the shore, stopping frequently at the little, red-roofed settlements, inviting little villas and sea-bathing resorts, to let off more passengers, for everybody in Copenhagen who can, must lie on the Strandvej for at least a part of every summer, enjoying the out-of-doors amusements, the bathing, the woods, sea, sky and sunshine. Nestling among the trees of the Strandvej, for miles, were little white, yellow, and green villas, among them Fru Ingemann's,—at the sight of which Karen, who always felt a little sick on the water, brightened, and exclaimed:

"There, Karl, is ours! You must come back and spend another summer with us up there. We do have the best times, don't we, Valdemar?"

The afternoon was singularly fine. Hundreds of ships were gliding silently past them in one continuous procession.

"Why," exclaimed Karl, "there must be the flags of every nation on the globe. I've counted the Russian, German, French, English, Swedish, Norwegian, Italian, Greek, Spanish and Portuguese flags, and, look!—there is a steamer with our dear old United States flag! How narrow the sound is growing, Aunt Else. The mountains of Sweden look nearer and nearer. I believe that, if I yelled loud enough, the people over there could easily hear me."

"Yes, Karl, we must be nearing Helsingör, for the Sound certainly is narrowing rapidly. It is less than two miles wide at that point. It hardly seems three hours since we left Copenhagen," remarked Fru Ingemann.

"Oh, mother, look! Isn't that old Kronborg now?" exclaimed Valdemar. "That is surely Hamlet's Castle, mother! Helsingör is where we land!"

"Yes, it is grim old Kronborg Castle, Valdemar. Many a tale its old gray walls could tell of terrible fighting, royal merrymaking, and of sadness. Karen and you, boys, shall go all through it when we land. For three hundred years Kronborg was the key to the Sound, keeping a sentry-like guard over the gate between the Baltic and the North Sea. For before the Kiel Canal was cut, as many as twenty thousand ships every year passed through this narrow strait, bound for Russian and Swedish ports; and Denmark grew rich from the Sound dues she collected. Now, the gates are open to the ships of all countries, and, when foreign sovereigns or men-of-war glide through this narrow silvery streak dividing Sweden and Denmark, old Kronborg's cannon give a friendly salute. But, come, we are landing now."

It was but a few minutes' walk up to the frowning old fortress on the promontory, with its many lofty, gray stone towers rising from the castellated roof. Karl was seeing for the first time in all his life a real "fairy-tale" castle, surrounded by a broad moat and ramparts.

First they were shown the apartments occupied by the royal family when, at rare times, they visit Kronborg. Passing a little chapel, with its carved choir-stalls and pulpit, they found themselves, after a fatiguing ascent, out upon the flat roof of a great square tower, fromwhich they gazed in admiration in all directions, for the day was remarkably clear and bright.

Far and near, over land and sea, the view was magnificent. To the east rose the mountainous Swedish coast, and, to the north, the gleaming blue waters of the Sound expanded into the equally blue Kattegat. All was still, like noon. Nothing seemed to move but the multitude of white sails silently passing and repassing through the narrow silvery strait below.

"Mother dear, do you think I shall ever be able to paint anything so beautiful as this? Uncle Thor could do it justice, mother; but I — "

"Yes, dear, if you work hard enough," was his mother's only answer, as she drew his coat collar closer about his neck, for a chill wind had risen.

"The Swedish coast is so near, mother, that I can see the windows of the houses," said Karen. "The coast doesn't look dangerous, does it, mother; but Valdemar says the guard told him he had seen as many as six shipwrecks here in one night."

"Yes, child, there are often bad storms on this coast; for the Kattegat is very rough and dangerous at times. Now we must go."

"But Aunt Else, I want to see the famous platform where the ghost of Hamlet's father walked that night," protested Karl, as the little party started down.

"Why, my dear boy, the ghost of Hamlet's father is believed to have paraded this very platform, right here where we are standing," laughed his aunt, as she put her arm about little Karen, who shuddered at the thought.

"Don't you know the familiar verse, Karl?

"'And I knew that where I was standing,

In old days long gone by,

Hamlet had heard at midnight

The ominous spectre cry.'

"This is, indeed, the far-famed castle of Elsinore, of glorious Shakespeare's fancy, Karl. You must, of course, have read about it in your school in Chicago," said Fru Ingemann, with a twinkle in her eye. "Through the magic of Shakespeare's great genius this out-of-the-way corner of our beloved little Denmark has become forever famous the whole world over. But come quickly, all of you; we have much yet to see this afternoon, before we take our steamer for Aarhus."

"Wasn't it here in this fortress, too, that beautiful Queen Caroline Matilda was imprisoned until her brother, George III, sent her to Germany, where she soon died?" asked Valdemar, as they hurried down.

"And, oh, Aunt Else, isn't it right here in this castle that Holger Danske stays?" demanded Karl.

"Yes, Valdemar, Queen Caroline Matilda was a prisoner here; and Karl, no one can ever see Holger Danske, although it is believed that he is alive somewhere down in the underground vaults of this fortress, and that, whenever Denmark needs him, he will arise and come to her aid. All little Danish boys know him. Valdemar, you tell Karl the story," said Fru Ingemann, as the little party hurried on.

"Well, Karl, Holger Danske is the great national hero of Danish tradition, the founder of the Danish nation, in fact," began Valdemar, who was thoroughly familiar with his country's history and traditions. "Holger Danske's cradle was a warrior's shield, so the story goes, and he sits down in the deep dark dungeon of this fortress, all alone, clad in iron and steel, his head forever resting on his strong arms, bending over a marble table to which his great long beard has grown fast. There he forever slumbers and dreams that he sees and knows everything that is happening above in his beloved Denmark. Whenever his country is in peril, or stands in need of his services, he will appear. But, every Christmas night, one of God's angels visits him in his dungeon, and assures him that all his dreams are true, and that Denmark is threatened with no extraordinary danger, and that he may sleep on again."

As they reached the Castle grounds, the guide pointed out the old moat, where Ophelia drowned herself, and the spring near by that bears her name. Then he took them to the grave of the melancholy Dane, in a beautiful shaded spot, marked by a moss-grown cairn of stones, and a granite shaft bearing the inscription:

"HAMLET'S GRAV."

CHAPTER V

"FAIRY-TALE" CASTLES AND PALACES

"'FREDENSBORG' means 'Castle of Peace.' It is an idyllic spot near here, famous the whole world over as the happy holiday gathering-place, every summer, of half the present crowned heads, majesties, and royal highnesses of Europe," said Fru Ingemann. "Let us take this waiting carriage now for a quick drive over there and back again in time for our steamer this afternoon to Aarhus. All this part of Eastern Zealand is so rich in romantic, fairy-tale castles and palaces, that I only wish we had time enough to see them all. But Fredensborg's hospitable roof has sheltered all the royal children, grandchildren, and great-grandchildren of good old King Christian IX, of Denmark, who was affectionately called 'The Grandfather of Europe.' Only think of a family reunion including King Frederik VIII and Queen Lowisa, of Denmark; their son, King Haakon, of Norway; former Queen Alexandra, of England, and her sister, the Dowager Empress Dagmar, of Russia, who were both Danish princesses; King George and Queen Mary, of England; King George, of Greece; and the Czar of all the Russias,—all meeting, every summer, in a quiet little family reunion in our obscure little Denmark at Fredensborg Palace!"

"But, Aunt Else, you left out the German Emperor!" observed Karl, who persisted in always mentioning the Germans.

"The German Emperor never comes to these royal gatherings, Karl. He is the only king who is not welcomed on Danish soil," explained Fru Ingemann, gently. "But here we are now at the palace."

They approached the palace through an avenue of magnificent old lindens, through whose interlaced branches they caught glimpses of the blue sky and of the still bluer Lake Esrom, near by. Then, entering a very stony courtyard, the carriage stopped before a few steps, guarded by two stone lions.

Soon they were walking through the apartments of the Queen, on the right, and of those of the King, on the left. From the King's plain working room, on the floor above, they looked out over the beautiful Marble Garden, so called from the elaborate statuary romantically placed among the old beech-trees, under whose deep shadows King Edward and Queen Alexandra, of England, did their courting. Nor was theirs the only royal love tale those mighty old trees could tell.

In one room still stood the historic old Settee of the Czar, so called because the present Czar's father, who loved children, used to sit there and play for hours with his own royal children, whom he loved so well.

Nothing interested them all more than the inscriptions — tender and pathetic — which they found on several of the historic old windows. Karl could only read a few, which happened to be in English, such as "Alexandra, September, 1868," and another, "Willie," which the King of Greece had written. But, when it came to a French inscription: "Que Dieu veille sur la Famille Royale et la protège.Alexandra, 1867," Karl had to call upon Valdemar to translate it for him, as well, of course, as all the Danish ones.

"'May God watch over the royal family and protect it,' is the translation of the French one, Karl, by Queen Alexandra; and Olga, Queen of Greece, has written in Danish here on this window: 'Danmark, Danmark, elskede Hjem,' which means: 'Denmark, Denmark, beloved home,' and here is a touching one by the late Czar: 'Farvel kjaere gamle Fredensborg,' 'Farewell, dear old Fredensborg.'"

"And, mother," said Karen, "here is: 'Farewell, my beloved Fredensborg. Alexandra, September, 1868;' and 'Christian-Louise, 1864,' and 'Valdemar-Marie, 1885.'"

They drove away through the royal grounds, which reached down to the shores of beautiful Esrom Lake, glimmering like a sapphire in the setting sun's soft light, and were soon back once more at Helsingör.

"Aunt Else," said Karl, "Fredensborg Castle looked exactly like the pictures of castles in the books of fairy tales."

"If that is what you like, Karl, then some day you must surely see Frederiksborg Palace, in the lovely forest region north of Copenhagen. It stands on an island in a lake, and is all spires, turrets and battlements, and certainly looks like a real fairy-tale castle," said Fru Ingemann. "Some of its venerable beeches are five hundred years old. But here is the little inn where we must have something nice and warm to eat before we take our steamer, in just a few minutes, for we will be sailing all night. We have barely time, if we hurry."

After finishing their little dinner of hot cinnamon-flavored soup, broiled fish, rye bread, preserves and röd-gröd, all of which tasted so good after their drive back through the woods, they boarded the little steamer which was to take them on their all-night trip over the Kattegat to Aarhus, on the east coast of the peninsula of Jutland, or the Continent, as the Danes call it.

"Aunt Else, on one of those windows at Fredensborg, was the inscription: 'Valdemar-Marie, 1885.' Won't you tell me all about the Valdemars? They were Denmark's greatest kings, weren't they?" urged Karl.

"Yes, but Valdemar will be glad to tell you all about them and about all the other kings of Denmark, too, Karl; but wait—here comes Fröken Johanne Nielsen, with her little nephews, Tykke and Hans, to talk to us. Fröken Nielsen is a great traveller. Children, don't you remember meeting them one summer up on the Strandvej?"

Karen courtesied prettily, while the boys arose, bowed, and politely gave their seats to the Nielsens. Then Fru Ingemann listened while Fröken Johanne, who only remained a few minutes, told them of the famous sights of Stevns Klint, or cliff, on Zealand's eastern coast, where they had just been; and of the still more wonderful scenery on the romantic little island of Möen, in the Baltic, where the dazzling white limestone cliffs of Lille and the Store Klint adorn the sea-coast, and where the summer-time sunset comes after nine o'clock, and the clear northern light lasts until morning.

"And don't forget about Faxö, Aunt Johanne, or Svendborg. Faxö was the best of all," put in little Tykke, as he delved deep down into his pockets and brought forth some pieces of fine coral.

"Yes, Faxö is an ancient coral crag jutting out into the Baltic," explained Fröken Johanne. "It is full of beautiful and rare fossils, and from Svendborg, on Fyen Island, we had such a beautiful view for miles and miles. From one high place the children could see alternate land and water five times, as well as the coasts of Sweden and Germany. The islands seemed like stepping-stones in the Baltic. But come, children, say good-bye; we must go."

While they had been talking the setting sun had thrown a yellow glory over the waters in front of Elsinore, which was now fading slowly away. The forests about the old castle on the promontory became dark, blurred masses, and the white sails below were mere moving shadows. The children could no longer see even the many fine specimens of fossils and coral which Hans and Tykke had generously divided with them.

The little steamer advanced upon the rolling Kattegat, with great flocks of white-winged sea-gulls following in its wake. Fru Ingemann noticed that Karen, who never could stand the churning motion of a boat, was turning perceptibly pale, and that a vague, uncertain feeling seemed to be creeping over even Valdemar and Karl, so she took her sleepy little brood below and soon had them all tucked snugly into bed for the night.

CHAPTER VI

THE LEGEND OF THE SACRED "DANNEBROG"

"IT'S a letter from Uncle Oscar, mother! I just know it is!" cried Valdemar, as Fru Ingemann opened and commenced reading aloud the only letter found awaiting them the next day, upon their arrival in the ancient town of Aarhus.

"And best of all," concluded the letter, "I have a great surprise in store for you all when you reach the Park next week. Karl will be especially delighted."

"Oh, Aunt Else, what can it be? How I wish I knew what father means!" exclaimed Karl, dancing about the room in anticipation of so soon seeing his father again.

"Let us make plans quickly," said Fru Ingemann. "I am wondering how we shall ever crowd into one short week all the fine trips and excursions we shall want to take before we leave here, for Fru Petersen tells me that the surrounding country is far more interesting than Aarhus itself."

"Yes, mother, the Riis Skov and the Marselisborg Skov, on the outskirts of Aarhus, are at their very best now for picnicking," added Valdemar, who always loved the woods. "A farmer passed us on our wheels this morning, and told us so."

"And he said we should not fail to visit the beautiful chains of lakes and fir-forests around Silkeborg," put in Karl. "He told us that Silkeborg was once just a manor, the property of the bishops of Aarhus; and that it came to be built in such a funny way. He said that one of the bishops was so charmed with the scenery in that part of the country that he took a vow that he would build a house wherever his silk cap, which a gust of wind had blown away, should remain. And so the strange name came about. Isn't that a funny story, Karen? Can't we go over to Silkeborg right now, Aunt Else?"

"Oh, not to-day, Karl, for it's much too late. Besides, the sky looks threatening. I thought I heard something like low, distant thunder just a moment ago. But to-morrow we can take an all-day trip over to Mt.

Himmelbjaerg and back, if we're all up bright and early in the morning," said Fru Ingemann.

They were stopping with the Petersen family, in a little red-roofed, many-gabled house on a quiet side street in Aarhus. Karen and her mother had taken a short walk through the residential portion of the old town and back, and the two boys had been out on their wheels most of the day, eagerly exploring every nook and cranny of the healthy little trading city on the Kattegat, which was a town of standing in the far-off days when Copenhagen was but a mere little fishing village. They had ridden past the Public Library, the artistic Custom-house, pretty little theatre, the interesting Art Gallery, with its fine collections by Danish artists, the grim old red-brick Gothic Cathedral, with its gables, narrow pointed windows and massive tower, and finally down to the busy harbor of Jutland's thriving capital, where large vessels enter, for it is built out on the open shore.

"Aunt Else, the other day, I remember, you called Jutland 'the peninsula;' Fru Petersen always says 'the Continent;' and once I heard somebody speak of 'us Islanders;' so which is it?" asked Karl.

"I'm not surprised that you are confused, Karl. I will try to explain it all to you," said his aunt. "Denmark is literally an Island Kingdom, for she has about two hundred islands in all, situated at the entrance of the Baltic. Since the cutting of the Kiel Canal, even Jutland, which originally was, and still is in name, the Cimbrian Peninsula, has now become in reality an island, some of whose parts, being actually below the sea-level, are protected by dykes and embankments. Even the Limfjord, which is no longer a fjord but a Sound, cuts Jutland in two again, adding one more to the list of Denmark's many islands. Even Copenhagen, Denmark's capital, is built upon two islands, — the great island of Zealand and the little island of Slotsholmen, over which it extends.

"Besides these, and many other smaller islands of the Danish archipelago, Denmark has colonies, much larger than herself, which, strangely enough, are all islands. One is Iceland, with its volcanic fires and geysers spouting through the ice; and the great snow-buried island of Greenland is another of Denmark's frigid possessions. There is also a group of islands in the West Indies.

".Yes, Aunt Else, thank you for telling me all about it. But I do wish I knew what father's 'great surprise' is to be!" sleepily murmured Karl, closing his eyes. "Valdemar, you were going to tell us all about Denmark's kings. Won't you do it now?"

"Yes, do, brother," begged Karen, as she yawned and buried her flaxen head in a big, soft pillow.

"Tell my best stories to such a sleepy audience? I guess not!" said Valdemar, himself yawning.

"Such a sleepy lot of children! Off to bed, every one of you, and up early in the morning," said Fru Ingemann, kissing them good night.

Hardly had they been in bed an hour, when a terrific thunder-storm broke over Aarhus. With the first deafening crash of thunder, the whole Petersen family sprang from their beds, dressed and rushed to the sitting-room, where they huddled around the great tile stove, their arms loaded down with their most treasured family possessions, Fru Petersen herself carrying the family plate and the cherished recipe book, which in Danish households is handed down from grandmother to mother and daughter.

The storm passed as quickly as it had come. By morning the ground was dry, the sky fair and blue, and Fru Ingemann and her charges well on their way to famous old Himmelbjaerg, which means Heaven's Mountain, for it is the highest spot in all Denmark.

"Why didn't we all jump out of our beds last night, too, mother," questioned Karen, as their train was passing through much low, hillycountry, in the midst of beautiful woods and lakes.

"Oh, that was just noget snak, Karen. The Petersens were brought up in the country, and they were afraid of fire by lightning. But here we are, Karl, in the scattered little town of Silkeborg, where the bishop's silk cap blew."

They first armed themselves with a large basket of provisions, then took a trim little motor-boat, which carried them past woods and gardens and picturesque little stork-inhabited farmsteads, up a pleasant river which soon widened into a lake, and then from one blue lake into another, on and on, until they finally stopped at the foot of heather-covered old Himmelbjaerg, on whose summit they could see a tall, obelisk-like monument.

"It's Denmark's Pike's Peak! Isn't it, Aunt Else?" exclaimed Karl in delight. "Father and I have climbed Pike's Peak in Colorado, and, I can tell you, mountain climbing is just lots of fun! Can't we go to the very top to-day, Aunt Else?"

With their long alpenstocks, Karen and the boys led the way up the gentle slope, while Fru Ingemann closely followed with the basket of good things to eat—smörrebröd, oranges, tarts, cake and sugar-plums, which disappeared as though by magic when they spread them on the grass in the shadow of the great brick tower.

The view from the "Kol," or top, was indescribably beautiful, reaching as far as eye could see over far-stretching forests, and valleys and corn fields and chains of lakes, in every direction to the unbroken horizon.

"Mother, mother! how wonderful!" exclaimed Valdemar, after he had looked long and silently at the impressive scene before him. "It's like one of Turner's great paintings!"

The grass on the mountain-side waved in the strong summer wind. Beetles hummed, insects buzzed in the heather about them, and a little field-lark, perched on a near-by beech-tree, poured forth its song, while Karen chased the brilliant-winged butterflies as they dashed through the sunlight.

"'Erected by Frederik VII,'" read Valdemar aloud, deciphering the inscription on the base of the brick tower.

Karen and Karl came running up, their arms full of mountain wild-flowers they had found almost hidden among the deep heather.

"Valdemar, are you going to tell us all about the Danish kings now?" urged Karl, who was a good student of United States history, and loved hero-tales of any country. "Please start at the very beginning. Karen wants to hear, too."

"And, after the story is finished, perhaps we shall have time for a little row on the lake," added Fru Ingemann.

Quickly they ranged themselves comfortably on the grass in the shade of one of Himmelbjaerg's giant old beeches, whose long arms swept the ground about them.

"Denmark means 'land of dark woods,'" began Valdemar, who loved his beautiful country, and was familiar with her legends and history from his babyhood up. "The Northmen were a fire-worshipping heathen people, according to Snorre Sturlason, who says that Odin, their chief god, was a real personage, who used to appear to men. But all this early history of Denmark is so full of legend, petty fights of kings, piratical exploits, and strange, wild stories and romances of the Skalds, that it is very hard to tell which is fact or fable, until we come to the last thousand years of Danish history.

"But in those early mythological days, when Denmark was covered with dark forests of mighty firs, Dan the Famous was one of theearliest kings, reigning in 1038 He became powerful, after uniting many small chieftains to himself, and so, according to some authorities, the country was called 'Danmark,' or the border of the 'Dans,' or Danes.

"Gorm the Old, in the middle of the ninth century, was really the first king to rule over the whole of Denmark, and his was called the Golden Age. His beautiful young wife, Queen Thyra Dannebod (the Dane's Joy), was full of goodness and wisdom, and after Gorm's death, she built the famous Dannewirke, a great wall that stretched across Denmark from the North Sea to the Baltic, for her people's protection against the fearful inroads and plunderings of their southern neighbors. One may see the graves near Jellinge, to-day, of Gorm the Old and Queen Thyra, two heather-covered, flat-topped cairns marked by massive old Runic stones.

"Then Gorm's son, King Harold Blaatand (Blue-tooth), ruled over Denmark, and was slain one night as he slept by a camp-fire, by the gold-tipped arrow of his heathen enemy, Planatoke. After him came his son, Svend Tveskaeg, who commenced the conquest of England, which was ended by Knud den Store, or Canute the Great, thus uniting the crowns of both kingdoms during his reign and that of his son, Harthaknud (Hardicanute), who was followed by King Svend Estridsen.

"Sometime I must tell Karl some of the wonderful tales I've read about all these old kings—tales re-told from the ancient Sagas and Chronicles, with their warrior-songs, giant-songs, hero-tales and ballads. Danish literature is full of them.

"But now we come to the three great Valdemars, and their glorious battles."

"And all about our Dannebrog—the flag that fell from heaven, Valdemar," broke in Karen, who never could hear that story often enough.

"And tell us all about the king who was put into a bag, won't you, Valdemar?" urged Karl.

"Yes, I'm coming right now to both those stories, which happened in the reign of Valdemar II. But first I want to say that it was Valdemar I who cleared the Baltic and North Seas of all the terrible Wend pirates, and it was also during his reign that Denmark's war-like bishop, Absalon, founded Copenhagen and gave the people a constitution.

"With Valdemar II a great and glorious era for Denmark set in. The old ballads and folk-songs tell how he courted Dagmar, the fair Bohemian princess, for his bride, and never was Danish queen more beloved by her people.

"Indeed, the Golden Age seemed to have returned to Denmark under the early reign of this successful young monarch, who was asknightly and handsome as he was courageous. His empire grew until he finally became master of Holstein, Schwerin, and all the provinces of Northern Germany, and his people called him Valdemar Seir (the Victorious). When the Pope granted him sovereignty over all the peoples he could convert, he set out upon a crusade against the pagans of Esthonia, with more than a thousand ships, and many thousands of men. With the Pope's blessing he sailed across the Baltic, but so vast did the host of the enemy appear, as his fleet neared the shore, that the Danes at first feared to land. But their archbishop reassured them, and they landed in safety. Towards evening, with King

Valdemar at their head, the battle raged furiously. The struggle grew fiercer and fiercer, until the Danes, who were outnumbered, were beginning to give way, when there arose a great cry: 'The Banner! The Banner!' Pagan and Christian paused. All eyes turnedtowards the sky, where, as though miraculously flung from heaven, was seen falling into the midst of the Christian ranks a blood-red banner bearing a great white cross,—our sacred Dannebrog. 'For God and the King,' cried the crusading Christians, as they seized the Heaven-sent flag, and again charged their enemy, who now fled in terror. The victory was won, and the Dannebrog, from that hour, became the sacred national standard of Denmark.

"Now I'm coming to the 'king in a bag' story, Karl," said Valdemar. "Denmark's power was now supreme throughout Scandinavia, Northern Germany and even over to Russia. Valdemar's reign was at its height. His people adored him. But there were secret foes—the conquered princes of Germany—awaiting his downfall. Among them was one in particular called Black Henry, who hated Valdemar, and was biding his chance to overthrow, if not to kill him. All in one single night the treacherous deed was done. Wearied by a day spent in hunting, the King and his son slept that night in a small, unguarded tent in the woods of the little island on Lyö. Suddenly their slumber was broken into by an unseen foe. The King could scarcely move, or speak, or see, or breathe. Black Henry had fallen upon King Valdemar and his son, bound, gagged and tied them up into two bags, and fled with his royal captives to a waiting boat in the river, and hurried them to Germany, where they were thrown into prison.

"Some years after, the King was ransomed by his loyal people with gold and lands, and he finally returned to his beloved Denmark amid the greatest rejoicing, to find most of his splendor gone. He was no longer king of a great empire, but he had his people's love, and spent his remaining years faithfully improving all the laws of his country."

"Oh, what glorious stories you do tell!" exclaimed Karl, who, with Karen, had been listening spell-bound to the end. "I shall never again see the famous old Dannebrog, without thinking of that wonderful story of how it fell from heaven, and saved the battle for the Danes."

"If Valdemar never makes his mark in the world as a celebrated sculptor, he certainly will as a great historian, with that memory of his," said his mother, indulgently. The afternoon sun was sinking in the west as they made their way down the mountainside, and soon left beautiful old Himmelbjaerg far behind.

CHAPTER VII

THE STORY OF THE DANISH "AHLHEDE"

SOON they were tramping past wind-tossed rye-fields and through sweet-smelling meadows from which, every now and then, a long-legged stork flapped its wings and flew skyward at their approach.

Their way to the boats of pretty Tul Lake,—gleaming through the trees in the sunlight,—lay along the banks of the Gudenna River, which has its source among the picturesque hills near Veile; then meanders northward through ranges of hills and green fields, winding with many a bend and curve on past old Himmelbjaerg, past Silkeborg and Randers, finally emptying through Randers Fjord into the Kattegat.

"Are you looking for the row-boats?" came a sweet voice just behind them. "They are just around the bend. I will show you the way."

Turning in the direction of the voice, Valdemar saw a pretty, rosy-cheeked, blue-eyed little peasant girl, in embroidered bodice and cap, carrying a great arm-load of poppies and forget-me-nots, and, stiltily walking along the middle of the road back of her, was a great white, red-billed stork.

"There are the boats now," she said, pointing down a wooded bank just ahead of them, and turning to go. Fru Ingemann offered her a small coin with her thanks and a smile, but the proud child refused the coin with an indignant: "Nej tak! Ingenting! Ingenting!" and started on her way,—the stork still following in stately tread.

"Is that your stork?" Karl couldn't help calling after her, for he thought it awfully funny to see the big white stork following a little girl in such friendly fashion.

"My stork? Why, no! I have no stork," laughed the merry-faced little peasant maid. "But there is a stork's nest on the top of the white church tower over there, and another one up on farmer Andersen's chimney, where he placed an old wagon wheel last year for them. And over yonder, in the eaves of the village houses, there must be several hundred storks. They are very tame, and often follow the plough in search of food for their nestlings, which they find in the newly-turned earth. This is their nesting time now. Then, when fall comes, they will fly with their little ones down to France and Egypt for the winter. But the same storks always come back. This same one followed me about last year. I think it knows me."

In Karl's land there were no friendly, red-legged storks stalking about the country roads, but he had read all about them in his "Andersen's Fairy Tales."

"Storks bring happiness and good luck," explained Valdemar, "and to kill a stork in Denmark is a greater crime, if anything, than to kill a fox in England."

As the boat moved out into the blue lake, through the silent reeds and water-lilies along the shore, with its drowsy white swans, Karl could still see in the distance the little peasant girl with her wild-flowers, the stork in the middle of the road still keeping stately pace with her. Then he burst out laughing at the funny sight.

Valdemar and Karl were both good oarsmen, and so they rowed far out across the lake, then drifted lazily along, while Fru Ingemann entertained them with one of Evald's charming fairy-tales, parts of Öhlenschläger's delightful "Aladdin," and tales from old Danish Saga-lore.

"Mother, won't you sing something?" begged Valdemar, who always loved to hear his mother's beautiful voice.

"Yes, while you are both rowing back to shore, for it is growing late," said Fru Ingemann, as she began and sang for them one of Weyses's old Saga-like romances.

The cool evening breezes, whispering among the trees, told them that the long, happy day was over, and that they must catch their train back to Aarhus at once.

Then came the day when they went by boat down the coast and sailed up Veile Fjord, to spend two happy days at the Munkebjerg,with many a ramble through the woods, guided to and from all the loveliest views by following the red or the yellow arrows on the trees, pausing now and then, after a stiff climb, to rest a moment in front of some little wooden chalet, or to sit and enjoy the scene from Atilla's Bench or Baron Lovenskjold's Bench, if they had followed the red route, or at Ryeholm's Bench or The Bench of the Four-Leaved Clover, when they had followed the yellow marks.

And from Munkebjerg they had gone to Jellinge, a town perched upon the breezy upland, and there they saw the two large, flat-topped, heather-covered "barrows," or graves, of Gorm the Old and Queen Thyra, of which Valdemar had been telling them, and Karl was surprised to hear that there still remained in Zealand, alone, some thousands of these Viking cairns, or Warrior's Hills, as they are called.

Then, as the end of their short week drew near, the children begged Fru Ingemann to take them by motor-car to Randers, where the famous annual Horse-Fair was being held, and they strolled through the streets of the cheerful old town, with its quaint old houses with their slanting roofs and protruding windows.

The Danish flag, with its sharp white cross on a blood-red field, fluttered everywhere. Hundreds of them decorated the exhibition field, to which the towns-folk and farmers, in their Sunday-best, swarmed, from far and near, to hear the speeches and witness the awarding of prizes to the superbly groomed, arch-necked horses of the famous Jutland breed.

The children had hoped to see the peasants still wearing Hessian boots and velvet coats covered with great silver buttons, but Fru Ingemann told them it was fifty years too late for that. They bought tickets—little bits of blue and white ribbon with "Randers" and the date printed on them—to the cake-man's booth, and there they bought all sorts of cakes fantastically made into queer-shaped men and horses and hearts, all covered with sugar and almonds and candies, each with a little motto on it.

Karen soon grew tired and sleepy, so they did not stay to witness the general fun and frolic and peasant dancing at night. As they left the grounds Karl, who was beginning to learn a few Danish words, exclaimed at an advertisement he saw on a signboard:Industriforeningsbygningen! "Valdemar, is all that just one word?" he asked.

"Just one word, Karl," replied his cousin.

"As we are all to leave Monday morning for the Park, and Randers is half-way there," said Fru Ingemann, "I have decided not to return to Aarhus at all, but to remain here over Sunday."

No one wanted to go anywhere on Sunday, so the day was quietly passed at home. In Monday morning's mail came a letter from Uncle Thor, asking how soon Valdemar could start up to Skagen, and also a telegram from Uncle Oscar, saying: "Meet me at noon, Monday, at Ribald. Pleasant surprise for Karl."

"Oh, Aunt Else, what can father's surprise be? I don't see how I can ever wait to find out." But his aunt only advised him to be more patient, for he would soon know.

"Tell me all about the Heath then, Aunt Else, and this Park, where we are going," said Karl, as their train sped rapidly northward through the low moorland hills, past clover fields where herds of fat red Danish cattle stood separately tethered; past prosperous little farms, some of them with their waving rye-fields, others all aglow with yellowing grain.

"Long, long ago," began Fru Ingemann, "in the days when Grandmother Ingemann was only a little girl, before there was any telegraphs or telephones, the very heart of all Jutland—as large a space as the whole island of Zealand—was just a dangerous, wild, barren desert, all sand and peat-bogs. The few Heath-dwellers who tried to live there led very lonely and dangerous lives. The Natmaend, a strange race of gypsy robbers, smugglers and kidnappers, wandered there. History records many dark tragedies enacted on the Heath. It was on Grathe Heath that young King Valdemar the Great met and overpowered his treacherous enemy, Svend; and, a century later, the Heath was the scene of a still grimmer tragedy, the murder of King Erik by Marsk Stig.

"The Ahlhede, or All-Heath, as the Danes called it, had not always been a desert-land, covered for miles with Viking barrows. There had once been beautiful forests of spruce and oak and fir-trees stretching over this four thousand miles of waste land. But what forests the long droughts and merciless west winds and cold blasts from the North Sea failed to destroy the ancient Vikings and their subjects cut down for their ships, huts and for fuel, leaving only a great silent, desolate, desert land. It remained thus for such ages that no one ever believed that it could be reclaimed, — that is, no one until Captain Dalgas set to working out his dreams and theories for conquering it. His hope was to win back to Denmark, through the conquering of the Heath, the territory lost through the Schlesvig-Holstein war. He formed the Heath Society and replanted the treeless wastes.

"To-day, countless farmsteads, meadows and pastures of the Danish peasantry dot the Heath from Germany to the Skaw. Trees again flourish; all has been changed as if by magic, and the plough goes over more and more acres of it every year, until a group of patriotic Danes, like your Uncle Oscar, have taken alarm lest all the breezy stretches of heather be reduced to farms, and none of the old-time Heath be preserved untouched for its own natural beauty's sake."

"Uncle persuaded a lot of Danes away off in Chicago, where he lives, to buy up a lot of the wildest and most beautiful part of it so that Denmark might keep it forever as a Park. Isn't that it, mother?" questioned Valdemar.

"Yes, exactly, Valdemar," replied his mother. "And, because of the untiring efforts of a group of patriotic American Danes, like your Uncle Oscar, a beautiful wild spot of three hundred acres up in Northern Jutland, near Ribald, has been purchased, and will be formally presented to the Danish government as a reservation, with the one condition that, every year, in that spot, when Danish-Americans cross the ocean to meet there and celebrate their Fourth of July on Danish soil, the Stars and Stripes shall float above Denmark's sacredDannebrog. Now that everything is ready, the Park is to be formally presented to the Danish Government."

"Presented to-day, mother?" asked Karen in surprise.

"Yes, this very afternoon. There will be a great crowd. Every steamer for weeks past has been bringing over hundreds of Americans, and, Karl, look out, for you may meet some of your Chicago friends among them."

"From home, Aunt Else? There's nobody I'd rather see from home than my own mother!" said little Karl, rather wistfully. "Gee! I do wish I could see my mother! I just wonder what daddy's 'great surprise' can be! Oh, just look at the big crowd!"

The train had stopped. "Ribald!" sang out the conductor. In a twinkling the car was emptied. As Fru Ingemann and her charges reached the platform, Karl saw two waving handkerchiefs making their way through the dense crowd towards him, and in an instant more he felt his mother's arms around him.

"Mother! mother! I'm so glad you've come!" he cried in joy. "Daddy, you did give me a pleasant surprise!" He laughed as Fru Ingemann and her sister Amalia greeted each other.

"Aunt Amalia, won't you stay over here in Denmark with us all summer?" urged Valdemar, as the happy little party was being driven rapidly on their way to the Park.

"Yes, Valdemar,—that is, I'm going to remain until your Uncle Oscar can get back from the United States again. That is why I have come—so as to stay with Karl, and let him see some more of Denmark, during his father's absence. And then I'm glad to see this wonderful Park, too, of course."

"Why, Daddy! Must you go back to America, and leave us?" protested Karl, who was having another surprise.

"I'm sorry, but business calls me back to Chicago at once, my little Karl. I leave this afternoon, immediately after the festivities, but I'll come back again soon. Here we are at the Park now."

As Mr. Hoffman, as president of the Danish-American Park, took his place upon the speaker's platform, and began his address, welcoming the thousands of American visitors he saw before him, back to the Fatherland,—to the Park—their Park forever,—a great cheer arose, which was redoubled in volume as the Stars and Stripes were impressively hoisted over the beloved Dannebrog—and then from a thousand voices the Star Spangled Banner floated forth over the Danish hills.

There were complimentary speeches by both the American and Danish ministers, and by Crown Prince Christian. Then every one sang one of those beautiful old national songs the Danes love so well to sing in their woods, and Karl told Valdemar and Karen the story of the "Birth of Old Glory," — as the United States flag is sometimes called.

In the evening, the whole forest seemed one vast fairy-land, with its myriad sparkling lights, strains of soft music, gay crowds and waving flags. Multitudes of lamps, of all colors and sizes, swung from the trees, throwing a romantic fairy-like light over the rustling beech-trees. Torches had been stuck wherever it had been possible to fasten them, and here and there a huge bon-fire flung its lurid glare over the whole scene, sending up great volumes of black smoke into the darkness overhead.

Three very tired and sleepy children were those whom Fru Ingemann put to bed that night, even before their usual time. The happiness of the long day — so full of new sights, surprises and excitement for Valdemar as well as Karl — was only marred by the leave-taking of Uncle Oscar for his long trip back to his home in far-away Chicago.

CHAPTER VIII

SKAGEN

TO Valdemar it seemed like a week, rather than just three days, since he had bidden good-bye to his mother, Karen and Aunt Amalia, and brought Karl with him up to the little painter's village of Skagen on the Kattegat, where they were to spend the months of July and August visiting Uncle Thor, who had built for himself one of the most charming of all the pretty, long, low, vine-covered homes of the famous Artist-Colony, of which he, as Court Painter, was by far the most distinguished member.

Up here was Uncle Thor's summer studio, with its row of fifteen great windows between which glorious red hollyhocks towered almost up to the red roof-tiles. On the south, the windows overlooked a gay, flower-massed garden where, on warm summer afternoons, the great sculptor loved to chat with painter-friends, and serve tea under his wind-swept old elms.

Here, in this bare and lofty studio, with its half-finished paintings and groups in clay, and, if the day be chilly, its crackling wood hearth-fire at the further end, throwing a flickering, rosy light over all,—here Valdemar was to spend many hard, long hours every day under his gifted godfather's instruction.

"In the whole of Denmark was there ever any boy half so fortunate?" thought Valdemar to himself, as he made a mental resolution to show Uncle Thor his appreciation by the hardest work of his life. Valdemar could work hard, and he meant not only to prove to his uncle what earnest toil and definite purpose could do, but also to win his offer to send him to the Academy in the fall.

On a low platform, in the centre of the studio, stood the unfinished statue of the little Crown Prince Olaf of Norway which Uncle Thor had commenced in Copenhagen at the Royal Palace. Day by day it was nearing completion.

"And here," said Valdemar's great teacher, uncovering a smaller but similar clay figure of the same charming subject, "is work my ambitious little pupil is to finish before he leaves Skagen. It will be hard work, Valdemar, and it will put your ability as a young sculptor to a fine test. But you can do it, Valdemar, and do it creditably, too!"

"Oh, Uncle Thor! Do you really think so? I'll try hard enough!" promised the lad as he set to work in good earnest.

The long hours, which Valdemar spent daily in the studio, Karl passed either out of doors or in reading all the fascinating books on Danish history in Uncle Thor's library.

There were frequent letters to both boys from Fanö, the little island in the North Sea, where Karen, her mother, and Aunt Amalia were spending the summer. Later they were going to spend a few weeks on a large farm, for a change.

And so the weeks passed. Finally Holme Week, with its clear, bright evenings, came; but the midsummer sun was growing uncomfortably warm even as far north as Skagen.

Valdemar's work on his little Prince Olaf statue was so far advanced that Uncle Thor readily consented when the two boys begged him to let them take the dog, Frederik, along with them, and tramp over the two miles of mountainous sand-ridges which led to Denmark's most northern point, Grenen, or the Gren,—a mere desolate sand-reef, the last little tip of Jutland's mainland, which extends between the waters of the North Sea and the Baltic.

The only signs of life the boys passed on the way, as they trudged along together, often ankle-deep in the sand, were a few long-legged birds, and several huge hares which shot across the road in front of them.

"We didn't bring along more than half the sand-hills with us, did we, Valdemar?" laughed Karl, as they threw themselves down on the beach at Grenen, emptied the sand from their shoes, and donned their bathing suits.

"Talking about sand, Karl, some day I must show you all that remains of an old Gothic church tower near Skagen. One day, during a service, a great sand-storm came up and buried the church itself so suddenly that the only escape the people had was from the belfry. That is all that can be seen of that church even to-day."

Frederik barked loudly and dashed back and forth after the two boys, who were soon bubbling over with the fun and excitement of dipping their feet first into the breakers of the Skager-Rak, and then into the waters of the Kattegat, the warm July salt wind and spray tanning their bare arms and faces. Then, Frederik following, Valdemar swam far out into the sea and back again, with the utmost ease. All Danish boys can swim well, and Valdemar wanted to give Karl a demonstration of his ability as an expert swimmer.

"Kattegat! Skager-Rak!" shouted Karl, who liked something in the sound of the words. "Grenen's great! But, honest, Valdemar, never in my life did I expect to bathe in both these raging seas at once! But here I go — look now!" and he plunged out into the breakers. Frederik dashed after him to make sure that he was safe, then came bounding back again to Valdemar.

"Ow! ow!" cried Karl, limping back on one foot.

"Crabber?" inquired Valdemar. "Uncle Thor warned us to look out for crabs and shrimps up here on the beach. You sit down here and rest, Karl. I'm going to gather some of those fine sea-gull's feathers scattered along the beach for you to take back home with you for your collection of Danish souvenirs. It was mighty nice of Uncle Thor to give you that letter from King Frederik!"

"And I'm going to put my shoes and stockings right back on again while you're gone!" said Karl, surveying his painful foot with a frown.

"Oh, look, Karl!" exclaimed Valdemar, as he soon came running back, his arms full of something. "Look what I've found for you! Sea-gulls' eggs! All greenish, with brown peppery spots on them, and here's a lot of the loveliest white wing-feathers, every one tipped with black! They're all for you, Karl."

"Oh, thank you, Valdemar. Let's blow the eggs. Do you know how?"

"Yes, of course. I've got a piece of wire in my pocket. You just run this wire straight through both ends — so! Then blow and blow!"

Together the boys had soon blown all the eggs, and tied them up with the feathers in a piece of old fish-net they found on the beach. Then Karl watched Valdemar while he made a hasty sketch of Skagen Fyr, the great white lighthouse towering above the sand-hummocks near the Signal Station, where it is said that every year seventy thousand ships are signalled.

As they started on their two-mile tramp over the desolate sand-ridges back to Skagen, Valdemar gave one last lingering look towards the wild, wind-swept stretch of endless beach they were leaving, where the North Sea and the Baltic have battled against each other for countless ages, with one ceaseless roar. Back of them, range after range of low shifting sand-dunes glistened in the sun, as they stretched towards the unbroken horizon in every direction. It was a strange new world to both boys.

"What are you thinking so long about, Valdemar?" asked Karl.

"Oh, Karl, it was off there that our noble Tordenskjold's little frigate, White Eagle, pursued the great Swedish man-of-war Ösel, and made her fly in terror. There's something about the very desolation of this place that, I like," said Valdemar. "Something strange, and picturesque, and romantic, I mean, Karl. One feels some way—up here at the Gren—as though he had actually reached the world's end! I'd like to come back up here often. Wouldn't you, Karl?"

"No! There's something I don't like one bit about it! I liked the Massachusetts Cape Cod beach at home; but that was different. I'd hate to have to live very long anywhere near here! Romantic isn't the right word, Valdemar. It's a lonely, wild, and forsaken spot, with nothing at all 'romantic' about it in my eyes. To me it feels like the 'jumping off place,' all right. And I've heard, too, Valdemar, that when a great storm is blowing, and the waves are rolling mountain high, that there are just terrible shipwrecks up here at this dangerous point! Down at the Skagen Hotel, the figureheads and name-boards, that they have collected from ships of all nations, tell the tale, Valdemar."

"That's true. There was the wreck of the Daphne, with the lives of eight of the brave life-saving crew lost. Sometimes there are twenty shipwrecks a year. But, Karl, this is the sea that made Vikings! Over these same seas, where our smoky steamers now pass, oncedanced Long Ship, Serpent and Dragon, with their gilded dragon-beaks gleaming in the sunlight! Can't you see them, Karl? I can! Uncle Thor has often told me the wonderful Viking tales. And I've read about their marvellous courage and daring. The Eddas and Sagas of the Vikings are rich in lore of those fiery-hearted warriors, who sailed over the stormy seas in their fleets of light ash-wood ships, conquering far and wide, and meeting death light-heartedly! They say some great Viking chief is buried near here. Their cairns and barrows by thousands cover Denmark to-day."

"Oh, I've read about them at home," answered Karl, who loved courage and bravery as much as did any healthy American boy, but who loved also to tease. "They were just a race of bold sea-robbers, and pirates, always 'hatching their felonious little plans,' always ready to burn and kill; and, according to history, some of the deaths they dealt out to their enemies were truly 'Vikingish.'"

"And yet, Karl, the ancient Sagas and chronicles tell that it was our brave Vikings who first of all discovered your North America, and founded a colony they called Vineland, near where your great Harvard College is to-day. The Sagas say that, five hundred years before Columbus lived, Viking Biarne sailed to America with his ship Eyrar, and that, later, Lief, a son of Eric the Red, went over to America, too."

"Yes, I know. I've read Longfellow's poem, 'The Skeleton in Armor,' and I've seen the 'Old Mill' at Newport, which was long believed to be a Viking relic," said Karl. "But we know differently now. Nothing has been really proved."

The sun was sinking in the west as the two tired, but happy boys reached the outskirts of the straggling little village of Skagen, andtrudged down the sandy road which led in and out among the fishermen's huts, with their tarred or heavily thatched roofs, and color-washed walls—some of them even built from wreckage.

Strings of fish, strung from pole to pole, were hung out to dry. Groups of sturdy fish-wives, here and there, with bronzed arms bare to the shoulder, and prettily kerchiefed heads, sat at tubs, dressing flounders for drying; and from the doorway of one hut came a voice so sweet and clear, crooning a quaint old Danish lullaby to the sleeping baby in the mother's arms, that the boys paused to listen as she sang:

"Den lille Ole, med Paraplyen

Han kender alle Smaa Folk i Byen

Hver lille Pige, hver lille Dreng,

De sover sodt i deres lille Seng."

"That was a pretty song. Tell me what it was all about," asked Karl, as they hurried on at a more rapid gait, for they were getting hungrier every minute.

"Oh, it was just a little folk-song every Dane knows. She was singing to her baby about the 'Sandman,' or den lille Ole, as we Danes say. She was telling him that the 'Sandman, with his umbrella, knows all about the little folks in town. Each little girl—each little boy—they are all sleeping sweetly in their beds.'"

They passed an old fisherman, mackintosh-clad, and another one in jersey and high boots, both hurrying towards the beach, where, in the gathering twilight, they could see a dim craft, a small fishing boat, with a few dark figures plying their trade, slowly rounding the promontory, its lights reflecting picturesquely in the water.

"Some day we must come back earlier, when more of the fishermen are home from their trips, and watch the crews at practice," said Valdemar. "These Skagen fishermen are true sons of the Vikings. It is said that there was one, once, who boasted of having saved two hundred lives."

"I hope you didn't worry about our getting home so late, Uncle Thor," said Valdemar, at the supper table that night.

"No, but here is a letter for you."

"Hurrah!" exclaimed Valdemar, as he finished reading it. "It's from mother. She says that Grandmother Ingemann has invited us all to spend Christmas with her down in Odense, and that Aage will be home for his vacation from the Military College, and be there with us, and Uncle Oscar, too, will be back again from America. Mother has decided that I am not to return to school until after Christmas, for she thinks that Karl and I are learning more by seeing our country than we could learn in school. And, best of all, mother says that I can remain up here studying with you, Uncle Thor, until September!"

"Hurrah!" said Karl. "No school until New Year's for me!"

"That means five more weeks up here with you, dear Uncle Thor!" continued Valdemar. "Now I can entirely finish the task you gave me to do, the Prince Olaf statue. I'm so glad, Uncle Thor!"

"And I'm glad, too, Valdemar, for you are doing me great credit as a pupil. I am going to be very proud of that statue of yours, Valdemar, when it is finished."

These last five weeks passed for Valdemar much as the first five had — in the studio.

"Study — diligent, earnest and honest," said Uncle Thor, "will win many honors for you when you are older, Valdemar. If you work hard, you should some day gather some of the roses that strew the path of the Danish artist, my boy."

"But once you said that Denmark was almost overcrowded with art students, Uncle Thor, didn't you?"

"That is true. But many of them fail to go on with their work; they lose courage and drop out. Others become interested in something else, and so leave their art studies. The few who do keep on usually learn all they can from the art schools in Denmark, and then go to Italy for further study."

"Yes, as you did, Uncle Thor, and as Thorvaldsen did, too," said Valdemar. "Oh, Uncle Thor! Do you think that, when I am older, I may ever be able to study in Italy?"

"My dear little Valdemar, anything is possible for you, if you work hard enough," was the great artist's answer.

CHAPTER IX

A DANISH PEASANT WEDDING

KAREN'S fair skin was tanned so many shades darker than her flaxen locks that Valdemar and Karl hardly knew her. Far down on the delightful Vesterhavet, on the sandy little island of Fanö, she had spent the happy summer-time with her mother and Aunt Amalia, first at the seashore, and later on the great farm of Peder Sörensen, near Nordby, where, most of the time, she had played out of doors in the sun and wind.

The merry harvest season had passed soon after Valdemar and Karl had arrived. They remembered how the harvesters had laid aside the last sheaf, decorated it with flowers and ribbons, and carried it in procession. Then had followed the great Höst Gilde, or Harvest Feast, a very festive function when sturdy men and rosy-cheeked maidens danced hand-in-hand.

Then, later, in the same beautiful month of October, had followed another folk-festival, and Mortin's Day, when in the evening everybody ate "Mortin's Goose," stuffed with boiled apples and black fruit.

Sometimes, on some of the children's many trips over to play on the beach by the West Sea, they had brought back pieces of amber washed up by the water. Karl found some pretty big pieces to add to his rapidly growing collection of Danish souvenirs, which now included not only the coral specimens, sea-gull's eggs and wing-feathers, but Fanö amber, and, best of all, Uncle Thor's gift of the great white envelope and letter from the Royal Palace.

Peder Sörensen was not a farmer himself. Like most of the men of Fanö, he was a sailor. It was the Fanö wives who, in their picturesque though rather unbecoming dress, cultivated the land, drove the cattle to pasture and the sheep to graze among the sand-hills, and it was they who milked the fine "Red Danish" cows at night, and made the far-famed "Best Danish" butter, with which they welcomed home their seafaring husbands.

Fru Anna Sörensen, who had studied farming and dairying at the Agricultural College, always presented a neat and attractive appearance in her dark blue dress with its one note of bright color down around the very hem, and her quaint red and blue kerchief head-dress, with its inevitable loose ends, which Valdemar graphically described as "rabbit's ears."

All the women of Fanö dressed just so, except, of course, upon some great occasion like Lowisa Nielsen's wedding, which was to take place in November.

Almost before they knew it, the short summer had flown, and November, with its cool, bright days, had come, bringing Lowisa Nielsen's wedding invitation, which the Bydemand, in white trousers, topboots, and a nosegay in his buttonhole, carried over to the Sörensens on horseback.

For propriety's sake, Fru Sörensen allowed him to knock a second time before opening the door, then politely asked him within.

"Greetings from the father and mother, and Lowisa, to yourself, your husband and guests," he began, as he took the proffered seat. "Your presence is truly desired at the wedding on Thursday next at ten o'clock. Come early, accompany the bridal party to the church, and hear their marriage service, return with them for dinner, remain for supper, then amuse yourselves with dancing and games the whole night; and then come again the next day, and take your places from the first day, and they will be sure to do the same for you when wanted from choice, on some enjoyable occasion."

This unique invitation being delivered, the Bydemand arose as if to go, but Fru Sörensen, with Danish hospitality, and according to an old custom, quickly produced a flagon of home-brewed beer, and a raisin-decorated wheaten cake, which she offered him.

As he finished the flagon and was about to leave, he turned at the door to add, as though an afterthought: "Then you must not forget to send a convenient amount of butter, eggs, a pail of fresh milk and two jars of cream."

"I will gladly," replied Fru Sörensen, as he departed.

On the wedding morning, at the appointed time, Fru Anna Sörensen and her guests, Fru Ingemann, Mrs. Hoffman, and the children, who had never seen a peasant wedding before, drove over to the great Nielsen

Bonnegaard, passed through the massive stone gateway, and into the open courtyard. They were graciously received by Fru Nielsen, and seated with the other guests upon wooden benches ranged around the walls of a spacious family apartment, whose polished rafters converged into a sharp-spiked peak at the centre.

Lowisa, a fair-haired, blue-eyed Danish peasant maiden, to-day looked unusually attractive, decked out in bridal array, — a pretty but tight-fitting homespun, escaping the floor all around by several inches. From Lowisa's richly gold-embroidered, tall scarlet cap, or "hood," as the Danes call it, hung pendent innumerable brilliant ornaments — round balls of metal and other fantastic dangles, all waving and twinkling as she moved. Extending from the back were vast bows and streamers of scarlet ribbon, under which she wore a head-dress of very rare and delicate lace. And the filmy white fichu, which crossed over her bosom, disclosed a rounded throat, circled by a bangle necklace of gold and silver coins.

As soon as the last guest had arrived, the whole party was driven over to the church, — the bride and her family in the forward "rock-away," the bridegroom in the next, then, in another, a band of rustic musicians, who, as soon as all the guests were seated in the different vehicles, struck up a lively air.

At the proper moment, the bridegroom, young Nils Rasmussen, a fine-looking fellow of true Saxon type, took his position beside Lowisa at the altar.

On returning to the house, the little church party was met by an eager, expectant company of guests, who had been invited to join them for the wedding-dinner. The bridal couple took their places at the middle of the cross-tables, which were arranged to form a square, after the fashion of ancient banquet tables, and, when all the guests were seated, the serving-maids brought in great bowls of steaming rice, and placed four to each table, deftly dividing the contents of each into as many sections, by making deep cross-shaped indentures, into which they sprinkled cinnamon and sugar and poured a cupful of hot butter. Then each guest, four to a bowl, lifted his spoon, dipped it into the delicious gröd, and began to eat. Meats followed, with wheaten cakes, highly decorated, and home-brewed beer of a very peculiar, rich, honeyed taste, and with the singing of a beautiful old Danish hymn the repast was brought to a close.

Then the room was cleared and the dancing began. It was certainly a beautiful sight, with every one decked out in festive attire.

"Nie tak," coyly refused each girl upon her first invitation to dance, according to an old law of peasant decorum, which also prevented the bridal couple, who led the dancing, from speaking to, or even noticing each other again during the entire festivities.

As the afternoon wore on the dancing continued. Between seven and eight, supper without rice was served, followed immediately by more dancing, which continued until four o'clock in the morning.

By ten o'clock the next morning the fiddlers had again arrived, and the dancing was renewed, this time with a noticeable increase in the number of rosy-cheeked, snowy-haired, elderly couples, in quaint holiday dress of homespun, with silver-buckled shoes. The bride continued to dance gracefully and bravely on, although paling cheeks told of her weariness.

Fru Nielsen explained that the third and last day would only differ from the first in that there would be fewer guests present, after which all would begin making formal calls upon the bride, which was considered the height of good form.

CHAPTER X

JUL-TIDE AT GRANDMOTHER INGEMANN'S

A FRESHLY fallen, deep, feathery snow covered Odense on Christmas Eve, and the merry jingle of sleigh-bells was in the air, as the little Ingemann party reached Fyen's prosperous capital.

Grandmother Ingemann did not live within the town itself, but a long drive in a big sleigh brought her Christmas guests within sight of the great old house with its many gables—all of the oddest stairway design—where most of her long, happy life had been lived.

Although it was only the middle of the wintry afternoon, darkness was fast gathering, and from many a window on their way a candle's soft glow shone out through the fluttering snow to guide the wayfarer to warmth and cheer.

"Welcome! and Glaedelig Jul!" called out both Grandfather and Grandmother Ingemann, who, in spite of the cold, had appeared on the door-step as the sleigh drew up.

"Glaedelig Jul!" cried Valdemar and Karen, kissing their dear grandparents, as Fru Ingemann introduced Aunt Amalia and cousin Karl.

"Where's Uncle Thor, and where's Aage?" demanded Valdemar as they entered the house. "And where's Daddy? Didn't Daddy come?" was Cousin Karl's first question.

"Yes, dear children, everybody's here," gently answered Grandmother Ingemann, smiling as she glanced out of the window.

Out rushed the children to welcome the sleigh that came jingling up to the door, out of which jumped Uncle Thor, Aage, and Uncle Oscar, just back from the States. Such huggings and greetings as then took place! Never had there been such a happy Christmas family reunion at Grandmother Ingemann's for long years and years!

Since his mother had last seen him, Aage had grown into a tall, broad-shouldered young man who carried himself with such fine military bearing—and preceded all his remarks with: "In my regiment"—that

Valdemar and Karl soon idolized him. And as for skating — well, he would show them something in the half hour, or so, that still remained before the time to start for the annual Christmas Eve service at the little church on the hill.

Then it was Valdemar's turn to receive compliments. Uncle Thor had great news! He announced that his talented little pupil's work had appeared at the Fall Exhibit of the Academy, — and had won a prize!

"A prize at the Academy! Oh, Uncle Thor!" exclaimed Valdemar, throwing his arms about his distinguished master's neck for joy. "Dear Uncle Thor! You didn't even tell me that my statue was to be entered at the Academy Exhibit this fall! Oh, I am so happy!"

Compliments showered upon him from Grandfather, and Grandmother, and from his own dear mother, and everybody, so fast that he was glad to make his escape with Aage and Karl, who were starting out to the frozen lake, with their skates.

Aage and Valdemar, like all Danish boys, were famous skaters. Karl was a fair one. Soon the two brothers were outdoing each other cutting figure-eights, hearts and arrows on the ice, and Aage even cut the face of his sweetheart. Then, as the music of a waltz Aunt Amalia was playing reached them, they called: "Come on, Karl, it's easy," and proceeded to waltz on the ice as gracefully as if on a ballroom floor. But Karl fell flat, and felt he had made a miserable failure.

Then they all came rushing into the house at the sight of several waiting sleighs at the door, which reminded them that it must be nearly time for the five o'clock Christmas Eve service. Soon every one was bundled into warm furs and crowded into the sleighs, servants and all, and the happy little procession made its way through the falling snow to the church.

As they passed through the village streets candle-lights gleamed from hundreds of windows, and here and there the children caught glimpses inside of brightly festooned little Christmas trees, and of sheaves of wheat or rye, fastened to the window-shutters out in the snow for the birds; and, strangest of all, Karl thought, were bowls of steaming hot oatmeal standing on many door-steps. But his mother explained to him that the bowls of oatmeal were placed there for the good little Jul-nissen, the Little People, or Christmas Nixies, the knee-high, little red-jacketed old men, with pointed red caps and long gray beards, who are supposed to form a part of every good Danish household.

When Grandmother's sleighing party entered the little whitewashed church, and took the places reserved for them, they found it already full to overflowing, and a crowd gathering outside as well.

The smiling priest in his dignified long black gown and deep-gauffered white Pibekrave around his neck, joined heartily in the singing of hymns and carols, which were re-echoed by the voices of the greater throng standing out in the snow. Then followed the Christmas sermon, and the usual touching prayer "for our brethren in South Jutland."

It was Holy Eve, the one night in all the year when services are held by candle-light, and the myriad wax candles, burning on the altar, threw a soft and mysterious light over the spruce and laurel boughs decorating the chancel.

The light snowfall had become a blinding snow storm before the little procession of sleighs had finally reached home, where the great dinner of the year was awaiting them, with its roast goose, stuffed with prunes and chestnuts, its cinnamon-flavored rice pudding, and a famous Danish dessert called Röd Gröd, the repast ending with nuts, Christmas cakes, candy and hot tea. Low over the table, illumined with a dozen tiny, candle-lighted Christmas trees, hung green festoons of laurel and spruce with a secreted sprig of mistletoe; while at every one's place were little mementoes, stuffed Nixies, snappers, and a small Danish flag, — except at Uncle Oscar's, Aunt Amalia's and Karl's places, where the Stars and Stripes were thoughtfully combined with the Dannebrog.

Towards the end of the dinner Grandfather Ingemann arose and proposed a toast to "our Danish-American guests," — whereupon all arose, touched glasses and drank, uttering the word for health, "Skaal!" Again, Grandfather Ingemann proposed the healths of "Our illustrious Court

Painter and his talented little pupil,"—when all again arose with their host, and the process was repeated. The last toast was "for our absent friends," after which Grandfather made a complimentary little speech, wishing every one joy in the years to come.

Then all withdrew to the drawing-room, where the lights suddenly went out, and the folding-doors of an adjoining room were flung wide, where, in dazzling beauty, its topmost boughs brushing the rafters, stood the great Jule-tree. Then every one formed a circle around the tree, and Grandfather distributed a basket of hymn books, from which all joined in singing that beautiful old Danish carol, "A Child is Born in Bethlehem."

Then, to the soft notes of a violin, all joined hands again, and slowly danced around the tree, singing as they danced another beautiful old carol. The servants were then called in, and Grandfather Ingemann called off the names, and distributed the presents. There were so many gifts for every one, from little Karen up to Grandfather Ingemann himself, that the floor was soon covered deep with the tissue-paper wrappings.

When the laughter and merrymaking had reached its height, there came a sharp ring at the door-bell, so sharp that every one paused in strange expectation, and little Karen rushed to the door after the maid. In the fast-falling snow stood a tall man in a green uniform and a three-cornered hat, who handed a great white envelope to the servant, with the words: "To Valdemar Ingemann, from his Majesty, King Frederik," then quickly departed.

Karen rushed breathlessly back to her mother ahead of the serving-maid. "Oh, mother! It was the King's Jaeger! Valdemar, it's for you! For you!" she cried, as the awe-stricken maid put into the boy's hands the great white envelope inscribed with the words: "To Valdemar Ingemann, from his Majesty, the King."

Every one looked inquiringly at every one else, but in the Court Painter's eye there lurked a knowing twinkle.

"Oh, mother! mother! Oh, Uncle Thor!" excitedly exclaimed the little artist, dancing about the room. "It's from my friend the King! He says he has visited the Academy and seen with great pleasure my statue of little Prince Olaf of Norway. He congratulates me upon winning a prize, and, mother dear, he wants to see me at the Palace, Thursday, at one!"

Even before Twelfth Night had come and gone, the American relatives had said their good-byes to Copenhagen and to the Ingemanns, and sailed for New York. Valdemar, accompanied by his Uncle Thor, had made the call at the Palace, and been entered as a student at the Academy, with the King's promise to him of long years of study in Rome just as soon as he was ready for it. So we too will bid good-bye to our ambitious little Danish Cousin, with his rose-colored dreams of the future.

THE END.